MW00884158

Wicked Mafia Prince

www.annikamartinbooks.com
Cover art: Bookbeautiful
Book Layout ©2013 BookDesignTemplates.com

Wicked Mafia Prince/ Annika Martin. -- 1st ed.
ISBN-13: 978-1535404389
ISBN-10: 1535404388

WICKED
MAFIA PRINCE

Annika Martin

A Dangerous Royals Romance

To Mark

"Twisted, sexy and dark—Dark Mafia Prince is everything I love in a stay-up-all-night-can't-put-it-down read!"

~M. O'Keefe

CHAPTER ONE

Aleksio

The girls move around in their rooms like caged animals. They exercise, they pace, they pound on the walls. Some gesture lewdly to the cameras. Others act pleasant, thinking, perhaps, things will improve things for them.

This I doubt very much.

There are thirty Valhalla virginity auction feeds in all. I track them on nine monitors, most of which are split into multiple screens. The monitors sit in a row on shelves in front of the living room couch in my new home, like nine TVs.

I watch the feeds nonstop, recording them during the few hours that I sleep.

My brother and I need the location of this place. I can't allow myself to miss even the slightest clue.

The laptop in the center shows Tanechka and only Tanechka. She is dressed as a nun. She never turns her face to the camera.

I know it's her. I'll always know *moya* Tanechka—my Tanechka.

Always praying. Tanechka never falters in her one-pointed concentration. It was the same when she was an assassin.

She seems to be concentrating on an icon, as a nun would. Such fierce concentration. So very Tanechka.

The nun disguise is brilliant. If this were the old days in Moscow, we would laugh together about such a disguise, relish it like fine vodka.

When I remember us too much, tears stream from my eyes. It's gratitude that she's still alive.

It's shame for what I did to her.

I threw the woman I loved over the steep, rocky side of Dariali Gorge. That was how we killed traitors while we were down south working with the Georgian gangs. The animals below would eat their corpses and scatter their bones.

They showed me evidence that she betrayed our *bratva*, sold us out to die. And images that she betrayed me with another. I was nineteen. So full of rage.

So foolish.

I should have been the one to go into the gorge for not believing in her. I nearly jumped in during those dark months after.

So foolish. I wanted to die.

That was two years ago.

Now here she is. Even with her back to the camera, I knew it was her.

My Tanechka survived.

The joy and disbelief swirled fierce inside me when I first saw her. I didn't have faith in her two years ago.

I should have believed in her, even when all the world and all the evidence told me different.

Now is my second chance to fight for her.

Her real name is Tatiana, but we all called her Tanechka, and I threw her into the gorge, yet here she is, outrageous as the torch lily.

I would give her anything. I would rip my belly open if she wanted it.

Who is she working for now? What is her mission? She's been there for weeks. Why does she wait? Does she wait for backup?

What are you doing, moya Tanechka?

Tanechka has attracted the attention of many bidders. She has the cheek of an angel and glorious blonde hair— you can see it peek out from under the head scarf that she ties under her chin, traditional for a nun in Ukraine. Numbers on the screen below her webcam feed show the latest bid. The number climbs daily.

Everybody wants to have the blonde nun who won't stop praying.

Everybody wants to see her face. To destroy something beautiful.

Turn, Tanechka, I think.

Not that I need to confirm it. I know.

Back home in Moscow, we were so deeply connected to each other we often thought the same things, and when we didn't, we would read each other with the barest of clues. We would read people and environments in the same way.

Turn. Let me see your face. Let me see your eyes. I think I would understand her mission if only I could see her eyes.

But no, Tanechka stays at her pretense of prayer with her usual unwavering concentration. Back in Russia, she could train her scope on a specific doorway for hours, waiting for a mark to walk through. True as a diamond, Tanechka was. She could watch a doorway all through the night, long after my own eyes drifted closed.

I don't know why she'd wear a nun's outfit, pretending to be a captive woman whose virginity is up for auction, a helpless victim.

Tanechka is not a virgin and not a victim, aside from the day I killed her.

Though it seems she was not a victim even then. I shouldn't be surprised she survived.

She's there undercover, so she must intend to take down the Valhalla brothel. Taking down this brothel is precisely what my brother Aleksio and I are working to do.

But who is Tanechka here with? Has she gone vigilante? Or is another gang involved, with Tanechka scouting things? Six weeks she has been in this place, judging from the bidding roster.

Tanechka never approved of sex slavery. She would have hated staying in a place like this for so long.

It is strange, really, that she stays.

Valhalla is the top income source of our enemy, Bloody Lazarus. He runs the most powerful crime dynasty in Chicago—a dynasty stolen from my brothers and me. We plan to take much of it back from him, but we want nothing to do with a place like Valhalla. We won't just destroy it—we'll reach into the pipeline that feeds it and destroy everybody who has ever been involved with it. We will tear this operation out by the roots so that it can never grow again.

In M-1 Global, our Russian version of Ultimate Fighting Championship, the best fighters soften their foes with strikes to the body before going for the knockout. Destroying income sources like the Valhalla brothel is a body blow to Lazarus. Then we go in for the knockout.

Lazarus helped kill my parents and separate me from my brothers. I wasn't yet two years old when he helped to rip me from my family in Chicago and dump me in a Moscow orphanage.

I grew up with only the vaguest images of my life in America. I thought they were dreams, these images.

My older brother, Aleksio, found me just last year. Kiro, our baby brother—*malinky brat*—is still out there, lost. In danger.

I focus on Tanechka, so steadfast.

To destroy Valhalla, we must *find* Valhalla.

My role is to pose as a customer, a man bidding on these trapped girls. Aleksio and I decided that I would win one of the insignificant auctions. We chose a scrawny girl, Nikki, for me to bid on.

When you win an auction at Valhalla, they take you in blindfolded to claim your prize. Some say that Valhalla is not even in this state, that they fly you there, but Aleksio and I think it's here in Chicago.

Valhalla has thirty auctions running at any one time. There is a feed below the current bid price where you can read the messages that the men type to the laptops in the girls' rooms. Some girls write back in bad English. Some seem even to be practicing their English through these exchanges. Some ignore the messages.

Tanechka ignores them, but she sees them. They are right there in her field of vision.

She speaks English fluently. This is how we met; Tanechka and I were singled out by the *Bratva* leadership—the heads of our mafiya gang—for our fluency with English. We were chosen to work as assassins, often having to pose as Americans.

Whenever we were together, we spoke to each other in English or else in French. Always practicing, sharpening our skills.

Two overachieving killers, Tanechka and me.

I watch the screen. *What are you doing?*

I don't dare send her a message. There's nothing more dangerous than somebody trying to help you on an undercover mission when you don't want or need help.

Hard as it is, going about your business is the best help you can offer an undercover agent.

So I wait. I watch for clues.

My fake identity for the Nikki auction is Peter, a German software engineer. The Nikki auction that I am to win closes in five days, and Peter will win it easily because few want this young girl. In this way Nikki is perfect as our point of infiltration.

Nikki is kept in the basement. I know this because I've made maps of the relative locations of the women in the place by tracking their eye movements. I can tell when there are loud sounds there, and I track the directions of their gazes to get their locations. The servers will likely be located in the basement.

The Valhalla handlers force Nikki to wear the white dress of a little girl. Advertised as a virgin. Perhaps she is. But she is not so innocent; any predator could see that she is a predator herself, 100% hoodlum. She would tear a man apart. Even tied, she would find a way. She would bite your cock off, I think.

Tanechka could do even worse than that, but she remains perfectly in character, kneeling at her bedside. Bidding for the nun who prays nonstop is *off the charts,* as the Americans say. High six figures now. Maybe it will get to a million.

She closes in three weeks.

What are you doing, Tanechka? How are you alive?

I aim to destroy this operation from the inside out before Tanechka's auction closes. I didn't protect her before. I have a second chance now.

The plan: I go as Peter the software engineer to Nikki's room. They promise to turn off the camera when a customer comes to claim his prize. I will ensure this is done, of course.

I will not fuck her. I only need to get to the servers to plant spyware. We've decided that I'll request that Nikki be gagged and tied for me, so I don't have to do it myself. This will save time. I'll convince Nikki to tell a tale of how I fucked her. We'll hope that she's grateful enough to cooperate in exchange for her eventual freedom.

Hard to wait.

I force myself to stand. Sitting on the couch all day is not so good. I bring last night's pizza box and a few glasses into the kitchen, where I also have a monitor showing the Tanechka feed.

I should clean. After this is over, I'll bring Tanechka here. She always liked things clean and bright. She loved sunflowers and daisies and soft lighting from lamps.

Tanechka gets cold easily. She likes big slippers. Thick shag carpets.

Back in the living room I study her. Now and then the girls all cock their heads or change the directions of their glances in response to sound—a scream. A siren.

Only Tanechka stays still.

So often I picture myself finding this place and storming in. Going to Tanechka's bedside. Begging forgiveness.

What would she do?

I walk around to the back of my couch and study the screens.

I'm recording them, but it takes so many hours to review and catch up that I watch them live as much as possible. I look for anything. A hand with a telltale ring coming into view. A reflection on glassware that I can run through facial recognition.

I grab a barbell and do curls as I watch. Curls are good for keeping awake.

I cringe when I hear the knock at my door. Yuri. My best friend, one of the men I brought from Russia. I've been putting him off.

I cut the light on Tanechka's screen. He'll think I'm crazy, believing this is Tanechka.

Worse, he'll tell my brother Aleksio. They would pull me from this mission.

"Come in," I say.

He walks in, addresses me in Russian. "What are you doing?"

I nod at the barbell.

"Do you have your phone off or what? You're not answering."

I grab my phone and see that it's dead. "Ah." I plug it in.

"*Chto eta...*" He gestures at the monitors. He wants to know what's up with the monitors.

"Preparing," I say. "Confirming the relationship of rooms. I'm more convinced than ever that Nikki's room is in the center of the basement." I show him my diagram, the gap where I believe the server closet is.

"Well, you look like fucking hell." He switches to English with "fucking hell." More and more he speaks in English. He opens the curtains.

I squint.

"Aleksio wants to know why you missed the meeting."

"I'm getting ready for Valhalla." I move Tanechka's laptop down alongside the others so Yuri won't think it's special. "I've arranged the monitors according to where I believe they are, relative within the structure."

"Mmm." Yuri comes round and looks. In Russian, he says, "It's a simple infiltration. Do you need such a thorough layout?"

He knows I don't. My job is simple: get spyware on the server. If I can't do that, I'll get to one of the girls' computers. I wave off the question. "I'm hoping for a clue to the location of this place..."

"We'll know the location when you get there," Yuri says.

"Best to know it ahead of time."

He furrows his brow. "Does Aleksio think this is the best use of time?"

"What are you saying?" I sound belligerent. Unreasonable.

He comes near. "*Chto eta?*" he asks again. What's up?

Insolently, I grab a vodka bottle. Beluga, our favorite. "A Boy Scout is always prepared." Yuri loves the American phrases. When I remember it's morning, I put the bottle down.

"No, something's wrong." Yuri's looking at the monitors. I know the instant he zeroes in on the laptop with the dark screen. He sees I'm hiding something. Does he want to know what that something is enough to defy me?

When he makes his move, I pull him back. "Is this my operation or yours?"

"What's on the dark screen?"

"*Idi nahuy,*" I say. "Go fuck," it means in Russian.

"*Chto eta?*"

"I don't have to explain anything to you."

Yuri is fast for a large man, and he's been getting sleep, unlike me. No surprise, then, that he can shake me off and get to the screen before I can.

"A nun." He eyes me suspiciously.

"Satisfied?" I sit back down. "It disgusts me. Auctioning off her virginity."

"You don't give a fuck about nuns."

"Anything else?" I demand.

He turns back to the screen. And then he sees it. "Wait," he whispers. "Wait…"

"What now? Did you come here for a reason or…"

"Her hair…"

My heart pounds. *Does he see it?* "What?"

"Her hair. The cheekbone." He turns to me in shock. "She reminds you of her. This is why you watch?"

"Look really close, *brat,*" I say. He is not my *brat*—my brother—by blood, but he is a brother in every way. We came up together in the orphanage in Moscow before the men of the Bratva took us and trained us.

Again he looks. How can he not recognize her? It makes me crazy. I loop an arm around his shoulder. "Don't you see it? Look, Yuri. Look harder."

He studies my eyes instead. "What?"

"Look at her!"

He looks at her.

"Do you see?" I demand.

"What?"

"It's *her*."

He turns to me.

"Look at her, not me!"

"She's dead, Viktor."

"It's her." I kneel in front of the monitor. "She never turns. But I know."

"You haven't even seen her face?"

"I don't have to. It's her. It's her body. Her style of movement. Look."

He doesn't look at her. He looks at me—sadly. "It can't be her, *staryy drug.*" Staryy drug—old friend, he calls me.

"You think I wouldn't recognize her? She prays like that for hours on end. But I don't think she's praying; she's meditating. Remember how Tanechka used to do that? She would focus her mind before a kill. Tanechka's perfect icy calm. Look at the way her hands are. Do you see? I think she is doing a form of isometrics..."

He grabs my shirt collar and pulls me away from the monitor. "Listen to yourself!"

I try to push him off.

He's too strong, too angry. He shoves me to the couch, gets in my face. "Do you hear yourself?"

"It's *her*. You don't know her like I do. It's her."

"Tanechka is dead. You killed her. You threw her into Dariali Gorge."

"We never saw the body."

"Dariali Gorge, Viktor! A mile deep!"

"It's her." I push him off me.

"What do you think she's doing? Is she there to bring the brothel down?"

"I don't know," I say. "Probably."

"Think. If Tanechka wanted to bring this thing down, she'd bring it down. She has access to a computer in there. Tanechka could make five kinds of weapons out of a computer. She wouldn't kneel and pray. Tanechka kneels before no one!"

I stand and glare. I'm sure he didn't mean to put that picture in my mind, but there it is: Tanechka, big blue eyes, hair like sunshine, light freckles across her face, kneeling, looking up at me.

I swallow, pull myself together. "Perhaps she waits for somebody she has a contract on. Maybe even Bloody Lazarus. She loved to take advantage of her looks. Remember how she'd do that? Remember her white dress and high boots? Those clothes she'd wear for the fancy jobs?"

"*Brat*," Yuri says. "If she was still alive, you know what else she'd do? She'd kill you. She'd sink a *pika* right into your neck. She'd smile while she did it."

I shrug.

"Doesn't matter," he says. "It's not her."

"It's her."

"Prove it." He points. "Message her."

"A message," I spit. "She's undercover. I might as well put a bullet in her brain."

"Or a message could prove that it's not her."

"I won't endanger her. Don't ask again."

"You used to have those codes between you. What was that one—'coffee with ten sugars'—that meant, 'do you have an SOS?' Try it."

"Are you crazy?"

"That's not so strange a thing to say. That way, you could test whether she's Tanechka."

"She's Tanechka."

"*Blyad!* This is psycho."

"Look how she breathes. Remember how Tanechka would do that? She wouldn't breathe for a long time, and then this lift of her shoulders."

"You see a ghost."

We watch in silence.

"You see this woman with your eyes, but I see her with my heart," I say.

"Viktor..."

"If only she would turn, you would see."

He sighs. His attention goes to the other women in their cages. He points to Nikki. "That one's yours?"

"Yeah. She just sleeps."

"She looks like a *bednyazhka* from a little village. What is that in English?"

I shrug.

He looks it up on his iPhone. "Ragamuffin," he says. "Nikki looks like a ragamuffin from a little village."

"Perhaps."

After a long silence, he says, "It's not Tanechka."

I say nothing.

"Viktor—" He rests his hand on the side of my neck and makes me turn to him. "This is a ghost here to say that you need to forgive yourself. You had no choice."

"If I'd truly loved and trusted Tanechka, I would have fought for her. Believed her."

"Then you would have died too."

"Don't make excuses for me."

"*Blyad!*" he says suddenly.

"What?" I tear my gaze from Tanechka.

He's pointing at the curtains. Sunflower curtains. *"Viktor!"* He stands and walks all around, looking at the furniture. He picks up a fuzzy blanket and throws it across the room, knocking over a vase. "You're making a nest for her."

"I want it nice for when I bring her back here."

He goes to the front closet. I sigh, knowing what he'll find. Still, I cringe when he comes back and hurls the white leather jacket at me. It's identical to the one she used to wear when she wasn't trying to be anybody else. The Tanechka trademark.

I clutch it, regarding him defiantly. "It's *her*." I want to press it to my chest, but not in front of him.

I'm just so tired.

"*Brat*," he says softly. He comes and sits next to me.

I close my eyes and flash on her expression—the surprise, the shock, the terror—as I threw her into the dark gorge. Even brave Tanechka was frightened of death. She reached out to me, even as she went over, eyes wild, grasping for my arms, nothing but cold wind whistling below her.

I should've been the one to go over.

I hear him unscrew the cap from the bottle.

"It's morning," I say.

"Not for you." He drinks and hands it to me. I take it and drink. Together we watch Tanechka.

"I didn't believe enough in our love," I say. "I didn't believe enough in her."

"We thought she betrayed our gang. Our family. So much proof."

"Proof."

"Tanechka was playing a risky game. She betrayed *you* by not trusting you with her plan. She should've trusted you."

"Do not *ever* say she brought it on herself," I growl.

Yuri sniffs.

We had this argument hundreds of times in those dark months after I killed her. Me in my room, drunk. It was only because of Yuri that I didn't hurl myself into the gorge.

"You had to."

I pull her jacket to my chest. "I should have believed."

Yuri puts a hand on my shoulder.

"She's back. A miracle," I say.

He's silent for a bit. Then, "So many monitors. Is a lot to watch."

I sigh, feeling so tired. I'm glad I told him. I've felt so overwhelmed and alone, trying to keep up with the feeds.

"You're looking for clues because you want to get to her if something happens."

He's right, of course. "*Da.*"

"You're taping it, but if you're watching the taped feed, you miss it live. It must be hard."

I nod. "*Da.*"

"Do you want me to take over?"

I regard him warily. "You don't even think it's her."

He puts his hand on my shoulder. "Let me watch for you."

"You'd do that for me?"

"*Immeno.* Rest your eyes. I'll watch."

I show him how I have it set up.

If he sees anything, he's to note the time on the monitor or go back and do a clip grab. He knows how to do such a thing. He knows how to recognize a clue.

I watch him through bleary eyes as he gets up from the couch. "Where are you going?"

He grabs one of Tanechka's fur blankets and tucks it around me, and then he sits down. I close my eyes. "Don't take your eyes from the screens," I warn.

"I won't," he says.

I close my eyes and put my cheek to the smooth pelt. I can almost imagine her here, speaking softly. She's so close. Praying on the other side of a camera somewhere in this city, or at least in this world. The world still contains her. My heart thunders to think of it.

CHAPTER TWO

Aleksio

I text Viktor. I don't hear back. One hour. Two hours.
Three hours. Nothing.

I'm not handling this uncommunicative shit of his very
well.

I tell myself there's nothing wrong, that I shouldn't
freak out about him not texting back. He's just invested in
his mission, that's all.

I tell myself I'm used to being with him nonstop.

It's just that I miss him. He's my fucking brother, and
I've only known him a year.

Finding Viktor last year, coming face to face with him
in that gloomy garage in Moscow, and feeling that instant
bond of love, it was one of the best experiences of my life.

I held him to me—I didn't give a fuck that the toughest
Bratva guys were all around, bristling with weapons and
distrust of this crazy American bounding into their space.

So yeah, Viktor and I have been together nonstop
since.

And I don't like us being cut off. Don't like him distant.

He needs space, I get that.

But all these years I thought my brothers had been slaughtered just like my parents were.

But I need to know he's okay.

Viktor speaks English amazingly well, but he goes Russian now and then. *Brat*, he calls me. I love that.

When we talk about Kiro, he uses the word *bratik*. Baby brother.

Kiro was taken when he was only eleven months old. By fucking Lazarus and his boss.

Kiro is still out there somewhere. He probably doesn't know we exist. Every second that goes by that we can't find him, he's in more danger.

Bloody Lazarus wants to kill him. Must kill him.

I text Viktor again. Nothing back.

Of course it's good he got his own place. Good for Mira and me to have some privacy. And he's making important bonds with the American Russian gang. That connection is part of how we'll take down Bloody Lazarus.

Bloody Lazarus, who destroyed our family and controls the empire that is rightfully ours.

Bloody Lazarus, who is hunting our baby brother Kiro as obsessively as we are.

Mira calls me from the back porch. I go out and find her in the hammock we put up. We're living this secret suburban life, and it's fucking amazing and weirdly wholesome.

"Anything?" she asks.

"Still waiting. Sooooo…."

She screams as I climb into the hammock. I don't tip us, though. I fit right in. I'm getting some specifically not-wholesome ideas, but she's trying to read. I'm fine with that. I just lie there.

My phone pings. A text. I read it. A lead on the guy who might have Kiro. My whole mood lifts. "Fuck yes."

Mira studies my face. "Is it what I think it is?"

"Could be. It's not for sure—just a lead—but…"

She kisses me.

I call the P.I.

I haven't seen Kiro since the night our parents were slaughtered in the nursery where my brothers and I once played. An old hit man hid me in a dark cubby while it happened. He held me there, hand over my mouth, arms like iron.

Baby Kiro cried while it happened, waving his fat arms as blood spurted from our parent's necks. Viktor was there, too, a screaming toddler. Bloody Lazarus and his boss took them both away. I was just nine.

Viktor and I learned just last month Kiro was adopted after that. When his piece-of-shit adoptive father couldn't handle him, he dumped him in the wilderness. Eight years old. And not just any wilderness—the fucking Boundary Waters Canoe Area, a vast expanse of uninhabited territory stretching through northern Minnesota and Canada.

From the story we could put together, our baby brother lived wild until he was eighteen, when he was found half-dead and brought to a hospital with a wound in his leg. Completely wild. The bottoms of his feet so leathery they were like shoes.

It didn't take long for rumors to start—a handsome young man, completely wild. The media flocked to the area, salivating for photos. Getting rabid, aggressive. "Savage Adonis," they named him. Fuckers.

And then the whole thing was shut down and Kiro disappeared. The authorities up there told everyone it was a hoax.

We know different. We believe he was taken.

We got photos of the man who likely took him, and our investigator ran them through every database he could.

Nothing.

We were crushed.

But now there's hope.

My investigator speaks fast. The man who took Kiro from the hospital posed as a professor. He tells me that it made him wonder if the guy *had* been a professor in the past. His team personally visited every college and university in the Midwest, showing the picture around. And it paid off. A name. A location. That's what unlimited resources gets you.

I text a few guys to meet me at Viktor's. I can't wait to tell them the news.

We are going to find this professor. And Kiro.

It's noon by the time my main man Tito and I get to Viktor's northwest Chicago neighborhood, a hidden pocket that is pure Russian *mafiya* territory. We park a ways down, just a precaution. My ankle still hurts from an injury some weeks back, but I can walk. Run if I have to.

You'd think you were in Russia, to walk down the street, smell the food, hear the chatter. We find Mischa, one of Viktor's guys, on his stoop a few houses down, and he's talking to people on the street in the mother tongue.

People are tight here, and there are eyes everywhere. If cops or muscle from Bloody Lazarus's gang were to set foot in this neighborhood, everyone would know.

We get to Viktor's condo, a brownstone row house, and knock. Yuri opens the door and puts his finger to his lips. "Shhh."

He leads us to the living room where Viktor is sacked out on the couch, cradling a bottle. Instead of a coffee table in front of the couch, there's a wall of monitors set up on a bookcase.

"What the fuck is this?"

Again Yuri puts his finger to his lips.

"Be quiet? It's noon." I frown. This isn't like my brother. Viktor may be an impulsive hothead, but he doesn't drink and pass out in the middle of the day. I go to him, but Yuri pulls me back.

"Let him sleep," he whispers.

"What the fuck?" I whisper back, alarmed. I saw Viktor not five days ago, and he seemed...distracted. But okay.

Yuri stations Tito in front of the monitors and gives him instructions on what to watch for on the bizarre array of nine screens, then he pulls me into the kitchen.

"What's going on? Is Viktor drunk?"

"Sleep deprived." Yuri looks out the kitchen window. "More or less."

"More or *less*? Talk to me." I join him at the window and touch the curtain—every room is beautifully decorated. You'd think somebody obsessed with home décor magazines lived in the place. Well, aside from the insane shelf of monitors flashing captive girl vids. "Is this about Valhalla? I thought everything was on track."

Yuri says something in Russian that sounds like swearing, just from the tone of it. He loves Viktor as much as I do.

"He doesn't need to monitor them like he's the fucking Secret Service," I say. "He needs to win the auction and get in. You all have the tech ready to go?"

"That's not the problem." Yuri opens a cupboard and then another. There's a ton of food. Lots of sweet stuff. This is not the type of shit Viktor eats.

"What's up with all the food?" I ask.

Yuri just grumbles. "Follow me, Aleksio." He leads me out of the kitchen and up the wooden staircase to the bedroom.

The bedroom is also done up like a home décor mag. Like a fucking woman's bedroom. Yuri flings open the closet. And lets out of streak of Russian that's probably more swearing.

He pulls out a hanger with a white leather miniskirt, puts it back, and paws through the rest of the stuff. All women's clothes.

"Whose shit is this?" I ask. Viktor doesn't have a woman.

Yuri pulls more women's clothes from the closet—boots, skinny black jeans, a blood-red vintage-looking cowboy shirt with black embroidery, a floppy white hat, a faded jean jacket with flowers. A Ramones T-shirt. This last he tears off the hanger and tosses across the room. "Blyad!"

Okay, that word I know. It's their version of *Fuck!* "Talk to me, Yuri."

He turns to me. "Tanechka clothes."

"Tanechka." I narrow my eyes. "His girlfriend who died. The woman he…"

"Killed."

"I don't understand."

Yuri picks up the skirt. "She loved black boots. She loved cowboy shirts. This red shirt—she had this very shirt. I don't know how Viktor found these things. Perhaps online. If I look in that chest of drawers, Aleksio, we will see ripped tights. Faded T-shirts. A white knit hat with a puffball on top. Tanechka's famous hat." He picks up a red T-shirt that says "Gone Fishin.'" "Tanechka loved stupid American sayings like this."

He puts it down, and I see here that Viktor's not the only one who grieves for Tanechka.

"What has he told you about Tanechka?" Yuri asks.

"She was the love of his life. He killed her in some kind of gang honor thing, and it turned out—"

"That she was innocent," Yuri says.

"He can barely say her name."

Yuri runs his palm over a scarf. "Tanechka was part of our gang as much as I was. She came from the same world we did. She was trained as well as any of us. She was so— scrappy, I think you would say. Fierce and wrong. Very fucking dangerous, like a white tiger. We all loved her, but what was between Viktor and her..."

He goes to the dresser and picks up a necklace.

"They would send her of on jobs with Viktor. So many jobs, those two. Tanechka and Viktor would pose as tourists. The wealthy young married couple, so much in love. Very believable, because they were in love. They could get into any hotel, any installation." He picks up one of the boots, black with a shiny buckle. "Tanechka could make herself look like an American businesswoman or French movie star. But these clothes that Viktor has been collecting, these were her regular clothes. Very much a hoodlum, our Tanechka. Hair like starlight, Viktor would say. She loved white leather. He is collecting her clothes, Aleksio."

I pick up the cowboy shirt, not liking this.

"He almost didn't survive her death," Yuri continues. "I never saw him like that—so devastated. What her death unleashed inside him was wild and dark. He lived at the bottom of a bottle. I think if it were not for his ability to become so drunk that he'd pass out, I think he would have jumped into the gorge himself. We were helping a Georgian gang at the time. We traveled back to Moscow after that, and I thought he would feel better, but he felt worse. Some nights he would shake in my arms. His grief was so powerful he would vibrate."

My heart pounds. "I thought he was…improving."

"I thought so too," Yuri says. "But this is not a home, Aleksio. This is a nest he makes for her."

I suck in a breath.

Yuri fixes me with a dead serious gaze. "There is a woman in Valhalla. He thinks it's Tanechka."

"Hold on. He thinks he sees Tanechka in the virgin brothel? Is that what you're telling me here?"

"He sees a ghost in there."

"Are you shitting me? All this time?"

Yuri nods. "Did you notice on the feeds that there is a nun who prays?"

I frown, recalling the Russian Orthodox nun on the feed. Viktor had gone quiet when we first saw her. I'd thought it was about the impropriety of it. "Yeah…"

"He thinks it is Tanechka. It's true, she looks like Tanechka from the back. She has her bright blonde hair. You can see this…" He traces the edge of his cheekbone. "Her face on the side, the shape of it. She is very much like Tanechka from the back and the side, a little bit. He has not seen her face, though—"

"Wait—he thinks she's Tanechka, and he hasn't even seen her face?"

"Yes."

"He thinks the nun is Tanechka based on her back."

"He says it is her body. Her movement."

"But it couldn't be—"

Yuri hesitates just a moment. "I cannot see how. If you would see this gorge, the part where he threw her in...nobody would survive such a fall."

I scrub my face. All this time I thought he was just obsessive about doing the job. "How could I not have seen this?"

Yuri shrugs. "I only just realized myself. We've all been working on Lazarus's people. Making friends with the Russians over here. Taking the empire."

I start downstairs, cowboy shirt in hand. I'm angry he would've kept this from me. Worried.

Yuri comes after me and tries to stop me. I whirl on him. "You want him killed? We can't send him into Valhalla delusional. Chasing a ghost."

"You think you can stop him?"

I continue on down. Viktor is still asleep on the couch. Mischa's there, and he and Tito have dug into a bag of pork rinds with the help of Derek, another of my guys. I study the nun on the screen. "She just stays like that?"

Yuri comes to join me. "Most of the time."

"Doesn't she fucking sleep?"

"Sleeps on her knees."

I send Tito and Mischa into the kitchen to make coffee, and I go right for Viktor, hauling him up. He's groggy. "Wake up! When the fuck were you going to tell me about this?"

"What?"

I shake him, and he comes to, pushing me aside so he can focus on the nun.

"You getting a good look at her?" I demand. "Because it's not Tanechka."

He glares at Yuri.

"Hey!" I shake him. "Look in the mirror if you want to find the asshole in this room! Seriously, Viktor. You would keep something this big from me and Yuri? The two people who love you most in this world?"

He focuses in on me for the first time, and I can see the pain. How could I have missed it?

"We're your family. We're with you in everything. We're here for you."

His eyes look a little glassy.

"Brother," I say, letting him sink down into the couch. "Let us be with you in this. You're feeling a little crazy, I get it—"

"You do not get it," he growls. "It's her."

"You threw her off a sheer rock face. That gorge—"

"It's her."

"You haven't even seen this woman's face. How can you know?"

"It's her."

I look helplessly at Yuri, who shakes his head.

Viktor pulls away and sits. "The fact that she's able to sit there perfectly still—Tanechka was a master of stillness. And why would a nun avoid the camera? This is what an assassin does."

"You're registered for the auction. You can write things to the girls. Why not write to her?"

"No," Viktor says. "Making contact could endanger her."

"Not if you write one of your codes," Yuri says. "Or say something about Gorky Park. 'I want to take you for lemon ice in Gorky Park.'"

Viktor glares.

Yuri ignores him and turns to me. "Tanechka loved anything lemon-flavored."

"No contact," Viktor whispers. "I won't endanger her."

We all turn to watch the nun. She kneels at the bed, praying, in the small cell that's a parody of a nun's simple room, I suppose. "What's she holding?"

"Prayer rope. Russian nuns, they do this. Her hair was bright like that," Viktor whispers. "Blonde like inside a lemon peel. I wish she would take off her head scarf so you could see all of her beautiful hair." He rubs his eyes. "But I'm glad that she doesn't. These other men, they don't deserve to see all of her."

"Coffee with ten sugars," Yuri says. "That was their code. Viktor, just message her that and see what she does."

"No!" Viktor says.

Tito and Mischa come back in with the pot of coffee for all of us. Viktor pours loads of honey into his and stirs.

"Guys always write stupid things," Yuri says. "Nobody will think anything of it."

I click to read through the exchange archives. Men are always writing in asking her to turn, asking her what's in her prayers, asking her to masturbate, asking what she has on under the dark robe. When guys ask the lewd questions, the others jump to her defense. Some ask more G-rated stuff—where she's from, what her hobbies are when she's not praying, what she likes to eat. She has quite the fan base. Everybody's curious about the nun.

"You could just be like, 'I'd love to treat you to a ten-course meal,'" I say. "'And after, a coffee with ten sugars.' What do you say? Just type that."

"No!" Viktor says. "You never contact a person in deep cover!"

I nod at Tito. Viktor sees the nod springs up, but he's too slow. Tito and Derek grab him and wrestle him to the couch. Tito gets him in a headlock, Derek has him in an arm lock.

I grab his face and look him right in the eye. "You see what madness this is?"

"It's her," he grates out.

"Then why don't you even want to confirm it? Isn't that a little suspicious? So I'm going to do it for you, and then we're going to get the fuck out of here."

I go to the keyboard and type in the message. The ten-course meal in Gorky Park. The coffee with ten sugars.

When I'm done, Tito and Derek let him go. He draws near the screen, swearing in Russian, vowing terrible things, I'm sure. The message I typed flashes onto the screen below, and onto her monitor mounted on the wall to her side, well within her field of vision. She doesn't move at all.

"She saw it," Viktor says after a while.

"How do you know?"

"She is aware of all things in her environment at all times. Perfectly aware, but she will never show it."

"If it was her, don't you think she'd at least shake her head no or something?"

"She doesn't want to," Viktor says.

I sigh.

"It's her."

After a while I say, "We can't send you in."

He spins around with a wild gaze. "You have to."

"Look at you! I won't put you in danger like this."

"It has to be me."

"No. We'll set somebody else up to go in," I say. "A new person, a new identity."

"That will take weeks extra!"

"We wouldn't have lost this kind of time if you'd come clean about this. This shit now? It endangers the whole crew," I say. "How do we know you won't try to go to her? And ruin everything? And then we have to rescue you?"

"Because I wouldn't endanger her like that." He shakes out of my hold. "Trust me. I won't go to her unless I think she's in immediate danger. I promise."

I shake my head.

"Once we set up surveillance and start turning their people, I'll be able to understand what she's doing and support her, protect her. I promise, I won't run to her. I will not be a cowboy, *brat*."

I gaze into his eyes, wanting so bad to trust him.

"I love her. I would never endanger her. Or our crew."

I look over at Yuri. He tips his head, inclined to trust his old friend. I study the screen. The bid on her is in the high six figures. God, is it going to go to a million? There really are a lot of scumbags out there. "You promise me when you go in for Nikki, you won't suddenly be searching for the nun?"

"Unless she's in danger," Viktor says.

"Immediate danger, like a fire."

"I promise. I won't be fucked up," Viktor says.

"She's so high-profile, she'll be guarded. You get that, right?"

"Of course," Viktor says. "And you need to understand, if Tanechka wanted to leave this place, she would be gone. Tanechka can care for herself. She's up to something. Our success in bugging them and spying on their computers will only help her."

"Fine." It makes sense, and more than that, Viktor doesn't lie to me. Except by omission, apparently. "You missed my money-laundering meeting. I could've used you."

"I'm sorry," he says.

I close my eyes. "I need you back."

"I'm fine."

"Make me believe it, brother." I wave my hand around his place. "This is not making me believe it."

"*Brat.*" He gestures at the screen where the nun prays. "It's all good."

I sniff. "You know why I came over here? We have a lead on Kiro."

He straightens, eyes wide.

"A possible ID on the guy who took him. Guy named Pinder. Remember how he posed as a professor? This guy actually *was* a professor at some no-name school."

"You think it's him?"

"Two aliases, two death certificates, and three warrants for arrest on fraud and impersonation? I'm thinking yeah. The PI says he's got hunting land in northern Minnesota that's in some kind of legal limbo. I'm having our pilot fuel up."

"Kiro."

"Look at you. Drunk, exhausted, and like a fanatic. You should sleep."

"Fuck you," he says, and that makes me feel a world better. "A lead on Kiro. Why didn't you tell me?"

"What did I just do? Get your boots and jeans. We're taking two parties of five. Carlo and a few of the guys are grabbing supplies. It's a huge swath of hunting land to search."

Viktor glances at the monitors.

"We can shut these off, right?" I say. "If anybody outbids you for Nikki today, you can just put in another bid when we get back."

He goes to the monitors. I can see him struggling. He wants somebody to stay and watch Tanechka, but he knows he needs to show he has control of himself. He closes all of the lids, then heads up to change.

They're probably still recording. He'll review the stuff when we get back, and it'll get worse once we have audio and computer surveillance on the place, but he's torn himself away for now. That's a good thing.

CHAPTER THREE

Tanechka

I pray, kneeling.

This hardship is a gift for which I am grateful. Every day this hardship makes me stronger.

I pray until my knees scream.

Then I pray more.

Sometimes I feel rage, but I don't act on it. I simply allow it to rise and fall, just as the sisters at the convent taught.

The sisters helped me to be calm.

I'm stronger than rage, that's what they said.

I keep my attention on the love and compassion that Jesus with his shining face would feel for these women who are locked here.

I even pray for these men who treat us like cattle, shoving us, tormenting us, making the weak ones cry, frightening them with tales of what will happen to us the day we're sold.

I ignore my mysterious impulses to hurt our captors. This desire to fight all the time.

Maybe it's from my old life. I don't remember. Why would I want to?

I slide my fingers along my prayer rope, whispering. The repetition settles my mind and calms my soul. The repetition helps me focus my attention fiercely on the small icon affixed to the wall before me. It shows Jesus in his red robe covered in a green cloak. To my captors it's just a bit of wood that perhaps raises my value in the eyes of those who would buy me. To me, it's a window to heaven.

The sisters said my impulse to fight with people makes me special. It is the lion that guards the gate to heaven.

I have to get past this lion.

I will rescue these women, but I have to do it without violence.

CHAPTER FOUR

Viktor

We land at a small airport in a small city named Duluth. The last time we were through here, the hunt for Kiro seemed doomed. The investigator was not hopeful. I wanted to hurt him.

Now this lead!

We rent cars and drive west from there with enough hardware to vanquish a small army. I'm in the first car. Yuri rides up front with Tito driving.

I sit in the back with Aleksio, reviewing satellite images of the imposter professor's hunting cabin. This man, this Pinder, has hundreds of acres of wild hunting land. He's supposedly dead, but it's all very mysterious.

Our P.I. did good work. I am happy I did not kill him.

"If Pinder has done anything to our brother, I will make him eat his own eyeballs."

Aleksio frowns. Love has made him lose his taste for violence a little bit. "Maybe if Kiro is as wild as they say, maybe this is the kind of place he likes. Maybe this isn't sinister." Aleksio. Trying to stay positive.

I say nothing. I do not feel so positive.

Aleksio blows a puff of air from his lips, moving a lock of hair from his eyes. Mira once said he had the haircut of a teen idol. *It's just a haircut grown out,* he growled. They had a silly fight. Aleksio and Mira can have fun over anything, especially the little things. The big things are more difficult. She's a lawyer who hates crime. He's a criminal.

On some things they agree. Like shutting down Valhalla. They are powerful allies who make each other better, I think.

Tito thinks it, too. Tito is Aleksio's right-hand man. He has short hair that he dyes wild and bright. Americans love their hair.

Tito and Aleksio are like two hoodlums, and Yuri and I are like two military men. Our hair is short. Dark. Severe. We have dressed in cargo pants and camouflage jackets.

"We could have him with us in one hour. Riding between us," Aleksio says. "Assuming he'll even tolerate a car."

"Right."

A man we met with told us that when Kiro came out of the forest, he was wild and uncivilized. Like a savage, he said.

I look forward to meeting this brother of ours very much.

It is difficult not to check Tanechka's feed on my phone, difficult to disconnect from her, like disconnecting from my own heart. But Aleksio needs to see that I can be focused on this trip. It is not easy, knowing the live feed of Tanechka goes on, knowing she could turn her face.

But I show Aleksio the reasonable brother he needs to see. We talk about the imposter professor, this Harrison Pinder. We talk about what we will do to him if he's hurt our *bratik*.

The cornfields flow by. American corn, much of it harvested. It is autumn. Stalks dry in the field. This we see in Russia, but everything else is so different—the buildings, the feeling of the people.

I miss it.

Up front, Yuri is arguing with Tito over nothing. Like stags, locking horns.

"I'm sorry I didn't tell you," I say to Aleksio.

Aleksio is hurt; I see it in his face. "Why didn't you?"

I look at my hands. "I didn't want you to try and stop me."

"It's okay," he says.

"It's not," I say.

He regards me with concern. Love, even.

I squeeze my eyes shut, so ashamed. "I would give my own life to take back what I did."

Aleksio grips my shoulder. My brother—with me, no matter what. "Your gang had evidence that she was keeping secrets from you, that she was working for a rival gang. You saw her kiss your worst enemy. It's a lot to take. She *lied* to you."

"I know why she did it."

"Still, she lied to you. She made it look like she betrayed you and your gang, and when you found out, she let you think it."

As it turned out, Tanechka was playing an elaborate con to save her mother. Pretending to betray us when she wasn't. "I should have believed in her." I force myself to feel the daggers of what I did.

"You're not a psychic, Viktor."

I stare ahead grimly. "My faith in her should have been strong enough to withstand anything."

"Your gang, the only family you ever knew, *made* you kill her."

"I should have believed."

Aleksio squeezes my shoulder again as if to say, *I am here no matter what.* He is a good, strong brother.

Cellphone service is shit out on the iron range of northern Minnesota, but Aleksio and his guys have satellite phones. Planes, equipment, hired muscle—we have so much now, thanks to the money our father hid for us. As if he knew what would happen.

As if he knew we would return to avenge his death.

We leave our SUVs at the edge of Pinder's property, then trudge through the heavily wooded area.

The trees blaze yellow and red; the sky is a vibrant blue. Tanechka loves nature, loves being outside. She always noticed the sky. *Look at the clouds,* she'd say. Always telling me to look at the clouds or the sun or stars or something. Always looking up.

She can't see the sky where she is now.

"We could find him today," Aleksio says. "Today!"

I grunt. I do not have such high expectations.

It makes me angry that they took him to a mental hospital for being wild. A boy who grew up wild is not crazy. There were some children like this in Siberia.

Our brother would be twenty now.

Distant gunshots. It's hunting season, which is convenient, considering we are a group of men wandering the woods with guns, except our guns are very powerful. And we do not wear blaze orange. We ignore the "No Trespassing" signs and head in.

I would not want to be the one who tries to stop us.

The cabin we located via satellite is many miles in. We hike until we reach a ridge that's near enough for a visual.

I look through the field glasses, and my heart sinks.

You can see from the foliage alone that the place is abandoned. Roof collapsed. Tall weeds in front of the door. I hand the glasses to Aleksio without a word. He looks. Says nothing. Simply gets back on the satphone to Carlo's party on the west side of the area. "We'll go first, move in carefully," he says. "You watch, ready for anything."

"I don't think people are there."

"Could be arranged to look abandoned," he says.

I nod. Aleksio is a smart, careful leader.

We cast around for traps as we move through the trees and thick underbrush. Finding none, we approach the cabin itself and push open the door with a long branch. It gives.

Aleksio and I go in together, weapons drawn. The place smells of rot, mold, and dung. I turn on my flashlight. Papers all around. Warped husks of furniture with the stuffing pulled out. There are even a few small trees growing through the floorboards, straining up toward the holes in the ceiling.

A cage takes up half of the main room. The bars are heavy and thick, running from floor to ceiling. Inside is a sleeping pad, a broken toilet, and a sink.

A cell for a lone prisoner.

The door hangs open. The area around the latch is blackened, as if it were torched open.

"*Blyad!*" I walk right in, right through the cobwebs. I don't care. "*Blyad!*"

We search the place. There are dusty books everywhere—philosophy of the ancients, mostly. Some evolution, anthropology. Spiral-bound notebooks with the pages stuck together.

"Fuck," Aleksio says, reading one. "Notes. Like an experiment. 'Subject will rattle the cage even while the bars are electrified. Subject shakes bars until unconscious.' What the fuck? *Subject?*" He throws the notebook. "Fuck you!"

I pick up a chair and smash it into the iron stove again and again, until I'm holding only bits. Our brother. Kept in a cage. "I am going to peel Pinder's skin from his face!"

Kiro was here. Kept in a cage. He could see out the windows to the outdoors. Like a taunt.

It's Tito who finds the bloodstain on the floor near the cage. What happened? Is this Kiro's blood? Pinder's? And what are the torch marks on the door to the cage?

Yuri tosses me one of the philosophy books. There are little marks in the margins all the way through. I check another. They all have marks, horizontal lines and here and there, exclamation marks. "Did he read books to him? Marking his reactions?" Yuri asks. "Teaching him?"

Aleksio gives us a stormy look.

Carlo pulls up a map on his phone. "There's a little town down along the river, population 880. Whatever happened out here, it would've been news. People talk. There's a little diner."

Aleksio surveys the books and notebooks. "These could provide some insight, maybe." He has Carlo's team gather them up.

It's nearly dinnertime when Aleksio and Yuri and Tito and I arrive at the diner. We take a booth and order burgers. The waitress is young. Her name tag says Britta. Her first job, perhaps.

Aleksio smiles in the charming way that he has. "You been around here long?" he asks when she delivers our meals.

Britta smiles. "All my life."

"We were up northwest of here and came on this abandoned cabin that had a big cage in it," he says. "What's up with that?"

"Oh," she says. She knows it. "Yeah."

"And the door had been torched open, it looked like," Tito adds.

"It was this whole crazy thing. You didn't hear about it?"

"We're from Chicago," Aleksio says.

"It was crazy," she says. "This guy was keeping an insane prisoner in his cabin. For like a year, and nobody knew. It was like something on one of those crime shows. He wasn't from around here. Neither of them were."

Aleksio maintains his charming attitude, makes a face that mirrors hers. "What happened?"

"Nobody really knows fully. You would hear hunters talking about sounds and things from there, but this professor, he told people he had dogs out there. Nobody imagined he was holding a person. He'd come into town for supplies. He ate here once or twice, but it was before my time." She looks around, grabs a ketchup from one table and puts it on another, then comes back, barely missing a beat. "And one day, they think, he got too close to the cage, and his prisoner strangled him to death. Then the poor guy managed to call out and alert some hunters. It was right after bow season opener. He was lucky in his timing—any other time of year and he'd be locked there for good."

My pulse thunders in my ears. I'm thankful Aleksio is here to keep her spinning the tale. He nods. "They heard him?"

"Yeah. The hunters called the cops. Nobody knew this prisoner he'd been keeping was crazy at first. He carried on regular conversations from inside the cage while they worked to free him with a blowtorch. He'd gotten the body of the professor out of sight, dragging it along the edge of the cage to the wall, so they couldn't see he'd strangled this guy right through the bars, not that anybody would blame him."

Yuri catches my eye.

I grit my teeth as she continues. "A lot of it is sealed in records, but I heard from a friend of a friend that this caged man seemed completely normal until they got him out and start questioning him. Then he starts freaking out. He's just tossing the cops around like rag dolls, trying to get out of that cabin. He kicks through the closed door—I kid you not, he didn't even use the knob—he's just out of there like the freakin' Kool-Aid guy. Again, would you blame him?"

"I would not," I growl.

"Me neither," she says. "But you don't beat the shit out of the cops who just saved you. So he's running through the woods, and there was this manhunt because they didn't know what he was going to do. I don't know why he had to attack the officers. Yeah, you're locked up, you want to get out, but the cops are getting you out, right? But of course, he was insane."

I bite my tongue.

"What happened to him?" Aleksio asks.

"Well, they got him. They hunted him with tranquilizer guns—one of our regulars is a large-animal vet who works the farms, and he hooked them up. And then I don't know."

I put on my best American accent. "Did he get arrested? Sent to jail?"

Britta shrugs.

"How bad did he hurt those cops?" Tito asks.

"Oh, one was in the hospital. For a long time."

Aleksio smiles. "I'm so curious. I really want to know what happened."

"Hold on, I have food up." She heads around the counter and through a set of swinging doors.

I ball my hands.

Tito lowers his voice. "He's locked up. I can tell you that right now. He fucked up some cops? He's been put away."

Aleksio swears softly. Breaking a man out of prison is no easy thing, even for us.

She delivers her food and comes back. "Some people say he got sent to Stillwater, but no one actually knows."

Stillwater. A prison with a psych wing.

This is clearly the end of our information.

We thank Britta, pay our bill, and pile into the SUV. Tito Googles for reports. There are none. It's all very strange.

"We need the police report. That'll tell us what the fuck," Aleksio says. We look up the precinct roster and study the names of local cops. We email them to Konstantin, the old hit man who saved Aleksio. Aleksio thinks Konstantin might have a connection.

"It is public information, right?" I say. "We ask for it."

"Yeah, it's public, and we could ask," Aleksio says, "but I'm guessing they'll make us file for it—a Freedom of Information request. And what if the officials here are connected to Lazarus's people? Lazarus has eyes and ears everywhere. If he doesn't have this lead on Kiro, I want to keep it that way. I say we bribe somebody. Nice and quiet."

Konstantin gets right back to us—he doesn't have connections to the police here, but he thinks Lazarus does for sure.

"We could do an armed takeover of the police station," I say. "They would have nothing but a few clerks in a police station out here. Right? Easy to take."

Aleksio considers this. "Yeah, but if we didn't get what we wanted, Lazarus would definitely look hard at this place. And he has the reach to find things faster."

"And it's robbing a police station," Tito says. "There's that."

I snort. "You Americans."

Tito laughs. "Dude."

"No, this feels like a time to go sure and slow and smart," Aleksio says. "For Kiro."

Aleksio has a plan—one of the investigators we use writes history books, loves his dusty records. "We're going to send him up like he's writing a book on the area and have him file for several things at once, not single out the cabin incident. We'll have him file for every big incident report of this area for the year so they won't be alerted. It'll take a few days, maybe a week, before they let him go to the county courthouse and examine the records, but it's safest. Safest for Kiro."

"Unless Lazarus has this lead."

"I don't see how he could." Aleksio makes the call and gets the P.I. right on it.

We're silent for much of the drive home, all of us thinking about that cage. Kiro in that cage. Midway back to Chicago, Aleksio starts talking about the money-laundering heist. Another way we have to hurt Lazarus.

It feels good. I want very much to hurt Lazarus right now. If I can't watch Tanechka or rescue Kiro, I want to hurt Lazarus.

Aleksio thinks they run their dirty cash through a restaurant supply warehouse on the South Side.

I turn to him. "Say the word, *brat*. We could attack there as soon as we land. Make it bloody. Divert their attention."

"Tempting," Aleksio says. "But let's do the recon first."

I sit back, fighting the urge to take out my phone and check on Tanechka. I remind myself that Aleksio needs to see that I am not obsessed. I remind myself I'm recording the feeds at home, that I will see everything when I get back. Catching up on the feeds can be confusing and time-consuming when you're trying to watch them live at the same time, but I've done it.

After we land, Aleksio decides that he needs my help with recon of the warehouse. I know what he's doing—keeping me from watching Tanechka.

Fine. I go with him.

We drive by the restaurant supply warehouse owned by Lazarus. This is a run-down part of town. Many buildings vacant. Many windows broken. I take note of the entrances and sightlines all around.

Most interesting is the warehouse right next door to it. It has a broken chimney on top. A broken chimney is a good place for a man to hide while he studies Lazarus's money-laundering operations.

A sign over the door of this warehouse with a broken chimney says "Brenner Industries." Aleksio looks on Google and tells us Brenner is imported textiles. We head around to a door marked "Deliveries Only" and ring the bell. A elderly security guard opens the door.

Aleksio and I don't bother drawing on this elderly man; we just push our way in.

The man raises his hands. He knows what it is, what we are. The place smells of chemicals they use to keep the cloth free of moths and other vermin.

Aleksio says, "This is either your worst day ever or your best day ever. Which do you want?"

"Best day," the man says warily.

Aleksio makes the deal with him. He agrees to let one of our men go up and hide in the chimney and stake out Lazarus's warehouse. He and Aleksio discuss how they will get the other guard who works there to play along.

This elderly guard sees that it can be a good day for them both. They'll both be paid. The warehouse they protect will not be harmed.

CHAPTER FIVE

Tanechka

At mealtimes we're herded into a large room to eat. My sister captives here are frightened, most of them Russian or Ukrainian, but there are also Americans and several Vietnamese in our group.

I comfort them the way my mentor, Mother Olga, comforted me when I felt so lost. There is one girl, Anna, who used to only cry. It's dangerous to cry, because they send you somewhere worse. I would hold her hand, tell her I'd get her out. Keep her from crying.

Images of escaping, of taking these women with me, keep bubbling up from deep inside me. The images are violent and deadly.

I reject this. I am not a violent woman.

At times I am forced to dine with Charles, the man who directs this place—just me and him at a special table. The sides of Charles's head are shorn like dark velvet, and he has eyes so brown they look almost black. My skin crawls when I sit with him. I sometimes think he has no soul.

The convent sisters said to love your enemy, but it's not so easy with Charles. He disgusts me.

Then I remind myself that it's not for me to judge.

I'm a novice, not yet a nun, but in all things I try to act as a nun, following the examples of Mother Olga and the abbess of the Svyataya Reka convent. And of course, I follow the example of Jesus Christ, whom we imitate in all things.

It's my deepest desire to rescue these women—without killing—and then make my way back to the convent. Maybe then the abbess to ask me to join the sisters for real. I would wear the outer robe and veil marking me as a true ascetic and take a new name.

I would return to my duties with the goats.

Life was not easy in that part of Ukraine, uncomfortably near the Russian border; we would often find ourselves at the mercy of insurgents and fighters of all kinds, who would come and take our food.

There were times we had to flee for our own safety, nights spent huddling in the small outbuildings with what treasures we could rescue. This we would bear. As nuns we pray for many things, but most of all we pray for peace.

I try to remember to do that.

I can bear anything for myself, but it pains me to see how scared the girls here are.

I know what it's like to find yourself alone in a strange place. Bewildered, frightened.

Two years ago I woke up alone in a strange place with no memory.

My body was twisted on a bed of tree branches, cutting into my flesh, into my back and shoulder. My shoulder blazed with the pain of a thousand blades.

That's my earliest memory.

My second memory was of looking up at the blazing blue sky, a sky so bright and blue it seemed unreal.

So beautiful.

It came soon to me how lucky I was. I had fallen off the edge and landed on a tree jutting out from a cliff.

But when I looked down and saw the distance still below me, I knew that danger still remained.

I called out for help.

My call echoed. Nobody called back. Alone.

I remember nothing—not my name, nor where I came from, nor how I'd come to be on a tree halfway down that sheer rock face.

You never feel so frightened as when you don't remember who you are.

For two days I picked and slid my way down the sheer rock face. Battered, thirsty, clinging to rocks and roots, sliding, falling, the pain in my shoulder sometimes unbearable. Finally I got to the river at the bottom of the gorge. I followed the river, only stopping to seek shelter against the night. At times I had to swim, due to the sheer rock faces on either side.

I wore jeans, a leather jacket, and a T-shirt with the words "The Scorpions." I hoped it might be a clue to my identity; I later learned that this is a famous rock band from Germany.

On the fourth day, hikers found me and took me to a hospital in Vladikavkaz. They dressed my wounds and put my shoulder back into place. The nurses there tried to find my family by searching for missing persons on the internet. Afterwards they called the authorities. Nobody had reported me.

I knew how to speak both English and Russian, and I had a tattoo over my heart that said "Tanechka + Viktor."

Common names that meant nothing to me.

My body is covered in ugly scars that didn't come from the fall—fighting wounds, one of the nurses told me. Some from the bullet, some from the blade. My wounds frightened them. I wanted to tell them that I wasn't a bad person, but I didn't know even this for sure.

It was at the hospital I met Mother Olga, who had fallen ill visiting relatives. I would sometimes talk to her about how troubled and bewildered I felt, with no memories of who I was.

No place in the world.

When Mother Olga was discharged from the hospital, she offered me a place helping the mothers in the convent in the vast steppe in Donetsk Oblast. She had warned me of the danger there; some of the nuns had fled.

I went.

I fell in love with the once-grand convent, a gray stone edifice surrounded by rolling green hills. Half of it was bombed away in the past decade, and much of the stonework is in disrepair, but even in its ruined condition it's beautiful to me.

The nuns taught me to care for the goats. They were frightened to take them grazing too far from their home, but I wasn't frightened. Fighting men didn't scare me; it was my dark past I was frightened of.

Mother Olga and the abbess taught me to pray. I found it all quite pleasant, but I wasn't moved by any type of religious feeling until one day when I was out on the steppes with the goats.

I hadn't been sleeping, troubled by an incident in town when I'd wanted badly to break the nose and fingers of a Russian fighter who mocked Mother Olga. Out there in the grass, I accidentally dozed off.

When I woke up, there was a strange light blazing from a thicket. I went to investigate it and found myself scratching away dried leaves and dirt to uncover what felt to my fingers like a wooden slab the size of my hand. I brushed it off to discover it was an icon of Jesus shining up at me. I did not understand how this painted piece of wood shone so brightly.

The light seemed to blaze from Jesus's eyes and face, brighter than the sun and all the stars.

All I knew was that I was filled with such indescribable peace, just gazing upon his face.

This light illuminated the bushes and the faces of the goats who had gathered around me. Like lightning, but brighter. As soon as I was able, I carried it back to the monastery, running at top speed, eager to show the mothers, but the shine faded.

By the time I burst through the doors, I held nothing but painted wood, an icon like all the others, only more damaged and weathered, some of the paint off.

Had I imagined it? Dreamed it?

Mother Olga was excited. She told me the icon had been stolen decades ago and was thought to be lost forever.

The abbess arrived when she heard. She said, "The grace of God has come to comfort you."

It was then I knew I wanted to join them. I wanted to feel this grace and comfort for the rest of my life.

The fighters came soon after I found the icon.

I shook at the way the three of them forced us to sit and watch as they ate most of our food and relieved themselves on the rest.

Then they made us kneel before them and remove our veils.

They meant great harm—I knew it in my bones.

When one approached the youngest novice, a girl of fourteen, I could not hold myself back. Like in a dream, I stood. I told them to step back. To leave.

They laughed.

There were five of them and one of me, but I had the anger of a typhoon in me. I could hear Mother Olga cautioning me, but her voice was nothing compared to the hot blood roaring in my veins.

The men laughed and said I would be first.

I smiled. I allowed them to get close. Nice and close.

Something held me still. I stood frozen like a rabbit.

As soon as I felt breath on my face, that same something whirled me into action. Elbow to throat, knee to nose, foot to jaw, fingers raking into eyes, all in one flowing sequence.

I remember the shock in the leader's face as he looked up at me from the bloody floor among his dead comrades.

I relished his surprise as I crushed his windpipe with my boot. This nun he meant to have fun with. Not so fun anymore.

I went to the last one alive. That's when Mother Olga grabbed my arm. "Tanya!" This was the name they called me. Hers was an old woman's grip, but it had power. "No more!"

I forced myself to still. My heart pounded so fast, I imagined the whole countryside could hear it. It was with an iron will that I stilled myself and bowed my head. "Please forgive me," I whispered in Russian to the one still alive.

He just looked at me, terrified. Face bloody.

Looked at the novice nun who had attacked him.

I could have crushed a mountain with the effort it took to bow my head and ask forgiveness.

We had to drive him to a hospital a day away.

Thus I was forced to begin my period of being a novice over again. I was determined to never fight again. To become a nun.

One day some months after that, I was napping on a hillock. I woke up with boots pressed down on both my arms, like boulders on my arms, and a sweet cloth being held over my mouth.

I was unconscious before I knew it.

When I awoke again I was locked in a dark freighter container with two dozen other women, out at sea for some weeks. The virgins among us were brought here to this place with cameras and many little rooms. They tested the other women for virginity, but they didn't test me. They assumed the novice nun would be a virgin.

They let me keep my head scarf and novice's robe in this place. They let me keep my prayer rope.

I hate cameras or surveillance of any kind—a feeling from my former life that I don't understand. Nevertheless, I pray faced away, whispering the Jesus prayer.

One of the guards asked me whether I would like a cross for the wall. I told him I would prefer an icon, and he was able to get one similar to the one I found on the steppes—a little more modern, but Jesus wears the same colors and holds his hand in the same beautiful gesture. This icon serves as a window to heaven just the same as one covered with gold or lit with a thousand suns.

I don't think he got it for me out of kindness; I believe my being a nun makes me desirable to bidders.

Still I am grateful.

I'll find a way to lead these captive sisters of mine to safety.

CHAPTER SIX

Viktor

Aleksio makes help him with the money-laundering surveillance whenever possible. He thinks I need something to focus on other than Valhalla. Maybe he's right.

Still I watch Tanechka and track the feeds. I sleep perhaps a little more, but I have to watch her. Sometimes Yuri helps, sometimes Mischa. These brothers of mine understand.

When two weeks are up, I win the virginity auction for the ragamuffin named Nikki for a mere $2,678.

It's time.

The men who run the brothel told me what to expect: that I'll be put in the back of a van and blindfolded for the trip, which will last two hours. I'll be checked for transmitting devices, weapons, and anything else suspicious. I'll have a maximum of two unobserved hours with this Nikki, during which time I may do anything aside from striking, choking, maiming, or killing her.

I put in my request for her to be tied and gagged, and I meet the Valhalla van at the bus station downtown as instructed.

I wear a fat suit, a blond wig, and a fake tattoo on my neck. Aleksio teased me that disguises like this are so KGB, so Russian spy. In fact they are. Some of the old men in the Russian *mafiya* got their start in the KGB. We learned much from them.

I'm instructed to hold out my arms. They bring out the wand. Relief flows through my heart when I see the wand is the type we predicted they would use. The tools I've brought are hidden in my fat suit, encased in a pouch with a device designed to manipulate the waves and send them back in a format that tells the men that I carry no hardware or no transmitting devices of any kind.

I promised Aleksio that I would abort the mission if they tried with any other type of wand. It was a difficult promise to make.

I ride alone in the back of a windowless van. I take my blindfold off, tracking turns, listening to the route, forming a map in my mind. The trip takes two hours, though I'm quite sure we haven't left the metro area.

I'm even more sure of this after they blindfold me again and lead me out; the feel of the air alone tells me we're near Lake Michigan.

I'm led into a structure that smells of new lumber and taken downstairs, as I knew I would be.

We stop, and they remove my blindfold. I'm in a hall in a finished basement flanked by two men, both armed. Guards are stationed on each end of the hall, also armed. Gray carpet underfoot, fluorescent lights above. Tanechka could make a bomb of such lights.

I remind myself she doesn't need my help.

A manager of some kind with a thick white beard comes up and explains the rules to me. He, too, is armed. I nod, keeping my posture humble as I make my assessments: exits at either end of the hall, five doors on either side. I merge this with the map I created in my head from watching the girls.

Tanechka is up and over.

I can feel her. My soul orients to her as a flower strains toward the sun.

The manager tells me the rules in slow, careful English. He wants to make sure I understand. I assure him that I understand, I repeat everything back to him, working to get the full sense of the place before I'm sequestered away. Carpet all around is good. Everything muffled.

I remind myself of the promise I made to Aleksio—unless Tanechka is in danger and needs me, I will not leave the parameters of my mission. I'll plant the surveillance and get out. I will not go to her.

The burly guard shows me his watch. "Knock when you're finished. If you use the full two hours, you'll have a ten-minute warning."

He opens the door. Nikki is inside, tied to a chair as I'd requested, glaring up at me. She grunts and protests from behind her gag.

The door shuts and I lock it, though I'm sure they can come in at any time. The room is frilly. Part of the fantasy. It disgusts me. The soundproofing looks good, though. This will work in my favor.

I turn my attention to Nikki in her white dress, rage in her eyes. Even muffled by the gag, her insults come through. She calls me a disgusting pervert with a small dick and so forth. An American.

"This is the last time I touch you," I say to her. "Got it? But you must stay still."

She doesn't believe me. No surprise, but she'll see. I take the ear plugs from my pocket and stick them into her ears, no easy feat with her head moving so wildly. Then I take the pillowcase and put it over her head. She writhes around, screams muffled.

I ignore her and check the room for cameras, running my fingers along the molding and the fixtures. They promised no cameras, but one never knows.

I pull my tools from the pouch in my suit. The first thing I do is to turn on the beacon so Aleksio and the others can get the location. Next, I use heat imaging equipment to plumb the walls in search of a mass of electronic equipment. If the server area doesn't adjoin this room, my job is all the more difficult.

Ten feet down the wall to the west I pick up the telltale heat signs of servers.

Good.

I pull out my tiny circular saw, which runs from a battery pack. Very quiet. I move a dresser and cut a hole in the wall behind it. I run a cable through. I have only a rigid cable with which to maneuver a thumb drive into the port, something I practiced. Using these tools on the ends of rigid cables is like writing a message with a ten-foot-long pen. It takes me the better part of an hour to get the thing in.

When it's in, I text out with the phone I smuggled in. The hack is live. I pull my cable out. This is going well.

That's when I see her staring at me. She got the pillowcase off, and she knows now. Will she talk if pressed? Will she use this information to secure herself favors in this place? To secure her freedom?

I put my finger over my lips, then I finish my job. I wrap the cables, shove them into the fat suit pouch, and carefully replace the panel I sawed away. I use a kit to mix up a pigment of putty and swipe it around, then I replace the dresser.

Fifteen minutes left. I turn to Nikki. Again the fear comes into her eyes. I shake my head and remove her earplugs, but not the gag. "I'm your friend," I say. "Understand?"

She nods.

"You will say nothing of this."

She shakes her head no, yes, no, grunting, desperate to communicate.

I sigh and remove the gag. "Take me with you," she whispers. "You can do it. I can tell you how!"

I kneel in front of her. "If I take you with me, it means I rescue one person. But with what we learn here? We rescue everybody. And everybody who would ever be here."

"And I fucking care about that why?"

"Because I care about it," I tell her.

"Take me."

"Not an option," I say. "You have exactly two choices. You keep quiet about what you just saw and we pull you all out in two weeks, or you tell what you saw and you never get out."

She gives me a piercing look, and I know she's thinking about the angles. The third and fourth options. This is a type of girl I know well.

"You want to be a fool and try bargaining with these people?" I put my hands on either arm of her chair and get really close. "You think they'll honor anything? I'm your only hope."

She just watches me. She knows. She gets it. "I want to go home," she whispers.

I stand. "I watch you all. It's not so bad."

She glares at me. "Yeah, not bad for me yet. But I won't be in this room for much longer. I'm headed somewhere worse after this. An underground brothel and it's not nice like this one."

"We'll find you," I say.

"Thanks a fucking lot," she says.

I sit on the bed. We didn't think of where Nikki would go after this. They'll see her as having been used up. Her virginity gone. I can only imagine the type of brothel she'll go to now.

"This is the best we can do. We'll try and find you."

She shakes me off with curses.

"Did you meet the other women here?"

She shrugs.

"Have you met the nun?"

She snorts.

"What's so funny?"

"Her god isn't helping her much, is he?"

"No, he's not," I say. "How does she seem?"

"Um...like a nun," Nikki says. "I don't know why everyone loves her. Especially the Russian girls. All she knows is the Bible. She doesn't remember shit from her past."

"What? What do you mean?"

"The nun has amnesia. Like on a soap opera."

I feel the blood drain from my face.

"She doesn't remember shit until two years ago when she woke up in some tree on a mountainside. She only knows her name from a tattoo. She thinks Jesus is her savior." Nikki flips her dark hair from her eyes. "Some savior. I think she should go see Jesus for a refund, if you ask me."

Tanechka remembers nothing? A nun makes sense as a cover. But a nun with amnesia?

My heart thunders. All this time I imagined she was on a mission. That my hands-off stance helped her. That she could protect herself if it came to it...

"What does she do when they mistreat her?"

"Um...have you ever seen that bumper sticker 'What Would Jesus Do?'"

"What do you mean?"

"She's a nun, dude. She doesn't give a crap if they shove her around."

The room swims before my eyes. Does she not remember how to fight, then?

These men could do anything to her, and she wouldn't be able to stop them.

I put her in this place sure as anything the day I threw her into the gorge. *Predatel*, I called her. Traitor. Betrayer.

"And then there's what her buyer will do," Nikki continues. "Though my money's on Charles in Charge doing the nun way before that."

I stiffen. "Charles in Charge?"

"The psycho that runs this place. He makes her eat with him sometimes, like this sicko date thing. You know that movie where there's a devil boy and all the animals run away from him? Add twenty years and Axe body spray and you get Charles. Everybody wants the nun. The guard who let you in here with the beard like biker Santa Claus? We think he wants to throw up those black skirts too—they demoted him here to the basement. Who knew the hot blonde nun thing was so powerful with guys?

Everyone wants a piece of nun ass, and now here you come—"

"Enough."

I stand and look at my watch. Thirteen minutes. I gave my word that I wouldn't grab Tanechka unless she was in danger.

"She is in danger." I say it aloud.

Nikki begins again to speak, calling me Sherlock.

"Quiet—let me think."

Nikki quiets.

I pinch the sides of my nose. Aleksio and the gang are probably in the neighborhood by now. The plan was that I would leave the way I came, allowing these people to blindfold me and drive me back. Aleksio and the gang were to follow.

This is no longer the plan.

I go and put my ear to the door. "You said the guard with the big white Santa beard is obsessed with the nun?"

Nikki nods.

"What kind of guy is he? Would he do anything impulsive? Stupid?"

"Besides being a guard at a virgin brothel?"

"How obsessed is he? Does everyone think it?"

"Like I said, they moved him down off her floor. Didn't trust him around her. Seriously, what is it about a blonde nun?"

"She's up and two rooms to the right?"

Nikki narrows her eyes. "How do you know?"

I pull off my belt.

Her eyes go wide. "What are you doing?"

I peel a pair of plastic shivs from the inside of it. "It's your lucky day. You're getting out of here. You know how to defend yourself?"

"Fuck yeah."

"Tell me. Tell me what you can do. Can you shoot a gun? Be honest."

"You got a gun?"

"Not yet."

She gives me a slow smile. "I can shoot."

I cut the ropes from her wrists and feet. "Pocket these. We can't leave them."

"I don't have pockets but..." She loops the rope loosely around her neck and ties bits together and stuffs it all under her dress. Good. Obeying without question. This can work. I can save Tanechka *and* the mission.

"You ever hold up a place?"

She nods.

"Successfully?"

"Yeah," she says. "I was in the Lady Sixx. You know who that is? It's a girl gang."

"You ever shoot anyone?"

She gives me a look—steady and straight and right into my eyes. "I'm a hundred percent. Whatever you need."

Good enough.

"I'm going to break the nun out and make it look like the Santa guard took her. We'll make it look like you got lucky and grabbed your chance to escape."

"Why the nun? The nun's gonna be dead weight."

I eye her, turning the shiv over and over, an extension of my hand. "Maybe *you're* dead weight."

"Okay, okay."

"Santa beard is going to come and knock to warn me in two minutes. Will he come alone?"

"Yeah," she says. "But there have been times when the men don't want to go when their two hours are up, and then more guards come."

"We'll work fast." I draw a map of the basement on the carpet with my finger. Nikki helps me do the next floor and together we develop a plan. The girl's good; she's been paying attention to her environment, making plans of her own. She knows about a large duct. It's information that I didn't have.

We decide she'll hold the obsessed guard at gunpoint inside this room while I get Tanechka. I stress that her job is to hold him and keep him quiet until I'm back.

"I got it," she says.

I nod at the shiv in her hand. "You may have to use that. We may have to get bloody before this is over."

She smirks. This one won't lose sleep over getting bloody here.

"The gun is the last resort. Any noise will fuck up our escape."

"I got it!" she repeats, impatient.

I text Aleksio with instructions. He knows not to argue in the middle of a mission. I adjust my fat suit. I listen at the door for footsteps. Eventually the Santa-bearded guard comes. He knocks. "Ten minutes."

"I'm ready now." I jiggle the doorknob as though I can't get it open. I flatten to the wall, and when he opens it I yank him in and disarm him. I hold his piece to his temple while Nikki searches him.

She pulls out car keys. "Score," she whispers, smirking at him.

"You want to live? You cooperate," I growl at him.

The guard gives up the location, make, and model of his car. I tie his hands; Nikki stuffs part of the pillowcase in his mouth, barely hiding her glee. She gags him harshly, also with glee.

I let her keep his revolver.

I take the guard's cap and shirt and another ring of keys. These would be the keys to the women's rooms. I close the door behind me. I don't have his beard, but this will be enough. I know how to move in front of the cameras.

I beeline down the hall to the boiler room. Every feeling in the world swirls inside of me as I near Tanechka. I unscrew a vent in the ceiling duct, hands trembling. This is the duct Nikki told me about. She'd been saving it for herself, thinking to hide in it if she ever got free. I pull myself up to the upper floor, just under the hall. I wait out the footsteps, aware that my ten-minute window has gone to five.

When the hall is vacant, I push up. I go to Tanechka's room, hesitating at her door, frightened it might be her. Frightened it might not.

I unlock it and pull it open.

There she is, kneeling, just as she does on the camera.

Tanechka.

She doesn't look at me, but I know it's her as sure as I know the sun in the sky.

"Tanechka," I whisper, pressed back against the door.

She doesn't move.

If she recognizes my voice, she doesn't show it. I'm shaking, resisting the impulse to fall to her, cover her body with mine.

I want to rip out my bloody heart and lay it at her feet, destroy it in front of her as she watches.

She focuses on the small icon, a replica of the many you find in Orthodox churches back home. I address her in Russian. "*Eto ya*," I say. "It's me."

She remains mesmerized by the small portrait. She hears all. She waits. She assesses. So Tanechka.

I slide behind her, allowing the camera to catch just that Santa guard's cap before I press a piece of tape over it. Framing him.

Still she prays. I kneel beside her, trembling with joy and grief at the sight of her profile, familiar as vodka. It's her.

"*Moya* Tanechka."

She turns to me finally. I was prepared for anger, hatred. But she looks at me like I'm a stranger.

She doesn't recognize me.

It feels like being shut out from the sun.

"You're alive."

She simply watches my face.

I stare, falling into her pale freckles, the royal blue of her eyes. Just the line of her lashes makes me feel indescribable joy—*korotkiye resnitzy*—"stubby lashes" she used to call them. She would coat her stubby lashes in black makeup. I study the way her smooth, creamy skin sweeps boldly out to her broad cheekbones.

She turns away. My heart pounds as she moves her slim fingers across the knots of the prayer rope, lips moving, whispering the prayer. The blunt white scar on her jaw, like an old friend. I remember the fight. One inch lower and it would have been her jugular.

I lay a hand on her arm, address her in Russian. "I'm here to get you out."

"You know me?"

"Yes. I'm getting you out. We'll talk later."

"Are you getting the others out?"

"Soon."

"Not now?"

"Later."

"No thank you, then. I'll stay until they're all safe. I'll be last." She jerks out of my grip and resumes praying.

My heart pounds. We're running out of time. "We'll rescue the others—soon."

"I'll wait."

Tanechka. So stubborn.

I stand over her. "Forgive me." I kneel and take her neck, choking her out. She doesn't fight me—instead she reaches up to the icon on the small stand; she slumps before she can grab it. I hoist her over my shoulder and then pause. I sweep up the little icon along with her rope and get out.

I don't want to take these stupid things, but it's what the Santa beard guard would do.

She truly doesn't have her memory—the old Tanechka would've had me flat on my back if I'd tried something like that. I hold her tightly, the weight of her in my arms like coming home. I rush her down the hall and toward the exit. It's not easy, but my Tanechka will never be heavy to me. Never too much to carry.

Nikki is already there with her guard. The girl is good. She holds up a finger when she sees me—one minute until we get company.

The Santa guard's eyes widen when he sees that I have his nun.

"You're coming with us. Shut up and obey or we kill you," I say to him.

We head out the back, down a stoop littered with cigarette butts to a patch of scrubby grass. Valhalla is nondescript from the outside, like a small apartment building. Tiny windows set into dirty, pale brick. We run up the alley past more such apartment complexes. We are definitely still in the city.

I carry Tanechka like she's my own life. Our van screams up, and the back doors open. Aleksio hops out. "What the fuck, Viktor!"

I throw him the Santa guard's keys. "Somebody needs to drive the black 2013 Volvo out of here now." I tell where it is.

Yuri comes around, eyes wide. "What did you do to Tanechka?" he asks in Russian.

"Nothing." Gently as I can, I settle the unconscious Tanechka into the back. I don't want to leave her, but we're running out of time. "You ride in back with her, Nikki. She knows you. Be nice or we'll throw you right back." I shut the door.

Mischa comes around. He has control of the guard.

"It's really her!" Yuri says.

I can barely contain my heart. "Hit me, Aleksio."

"The fuck?" Aleksio's pissed.

"I had to do it, *brat*. I'll go back and sell it. The mission is fine. I'll go back and manage things. You'll see."

Yuri comes up and hits me in the jaw. I clip my lips into my teeth and make him hit me again so that it will be good and bloody—we've done this many times.

I grin. "Now get them safe." I rush around through the alley, making it back to Valhalla's backyard just as two guards are running out.

I act the part of the dazed, angry customer, demanding my money back. "Look what that ragamuffin did!" I say, gesturing at my jaw. "She hit me!"

I give them the tall tale. I tell them Nikki hit me. I say I called out to the Santa guard, but Nikki took Santa guard's gun and ran off. I tell them how the Santa guard seemed upset and angry and how he left me alone in the room. I called out and nobody came, so I went out in search of somebody. The outside door was open, so I wandered out, looking for the van, for a ride home. I play my part forcefully, with commitment, all in broken English and a little bit of German. I'm the angry customer.

The guards start putting it together, telling each other in their own words. "He let Nikki go and he knew Charles would fuck him up, so he ran," one of them suggests to another.

Then they find the nun gone. The story changes—Santa guard fucked up and let Nikki escape, and he had nothing more to lose, so he ran away and took the nun with him. They all talk about how pissed Charles will be.

I demand my money back, as though that's my main concern.

The story of the bearded guard taking the nun continues, gains more detail.

It's working. I'm relieved.

When I ask a third time for my money back, I get a Glock shoved into my neck. "How about we drive you back instead of killing you—would you settle for that?"

I put up my hands as they threaten my fictional family. If I reveal anything, they say, people that I love will die. I play it frightened, promising never to speak of it.

They no longer think of customer service with me.

They blame me a little bit, I think. After all, the chain of events began with me. I allowed a girl they tied and bound to hit me. I whined enough to distract the guard and allow her to steal his gun and escape.

They blindfold me and put me back in the rear of the van to take me back. I put my ear to the metal partition, straining to hear. They're upset with the Santa guard. They're hunting for him and Tanechka already.

Aleksio will put him somewhere. This guard will have good information.

Tanechka will stay with me.

The ride back to the bus station takes much less time. They don't bother driving in circles to fool me now that they've threatened my family.

We arrive back at the train station. They strip my blindfold off and nearly throw me to the curb. They have worse problems than me.

I walk through the crowded station. I don't think they're tailing me, but I'm always careful. I come out the other side and see Aleksio leaning against his Jaguar.

He grabs my suit jacket and slams me back against the door, eyes wild. "Were you always going to grab her? Just tell me. I need to know. Were you planning it?"

"No. I wasn't."

He twists my shirt, pushes me harder. "I need to trust you!"

"Where is she? Is she okay?"

Aleksio glares, nostrils flaring. "What the fuck? You shouldn't even get to see her now!"

"She's awake?"

"Yeah," he bites out. "She's back at the house with Tito and that girl, Nikki. Mischa's on his way."

I nod. She and Mischa were close friends. "She was in danger." I tell Aleksio about the amnesia. "I couldn't leave her."

"Was she in danger that minute?"

"That minute?" I look into his eyes. "No."

"So what the fuck?"

"She has no memory! She can't defend herself!"

Aleksio lets me go with a huff of disgust and swings into the driver's seat.

"You'd do the same for Mira," I say.

Yuri's in the front barely suppressing his smile. *Tanechka's back!* I get in the back seat.

Aleksio peels out, barely giving me time to close my door. "We need to be able to trust each other," he says.

"You can always trust Viktor," Yuri says. "But he will always put Tanechka above everything. That's the only thing."

"The mission isn't compromised," I say. "They still think I'm Peter the German technologist. They won't think I was there to set up surveillance. We're *good*."

Aleksio grumbles.

"I know how to set a man up," I tell him.

"If Viktor says he set the man up, he set the man up," Yuri says. Yuri always has my back.

"They wouldn't have driven me back if they suspected anything," I add.

Yuri points out that we now have a guard to question in addition to the intrusive surveillance.

"Fine, a live guard and surveillance is better than just surveillance," Aleksio says. "But Viktor. What the fuck."

Shivers slide over me. "It's *her*," I say.

Yuri turns and meets my eyes. "But if she really thinks she's a nun…"

"I don't care. It's Tanechka. I'll make her remember."

Yuri frowns. "I wouldn't want her to remember if I were you. Or at least make sure we're around. To protect you."

"She's alive," I say. "Nothing else matters."

CHAPTER SEVEN

Tanechka

The men take Nikki and me to a very nice home, a row house it's called, in Chicago. There's an American, Tito, in charge. He's big and burly; his short hair is nearly white on the tips.

The halo of a killer.

I may not have my memories, but I know a killer when I see one. Something deep inside me tells me. Like the man who took me out of that place—the man who knelt by me and seemed to know me. He's a killer, too.

I always worried that somebody would appear from my old life and endanger my sister nuns at the convent. I never imagined somebody from my old life would find me in that brothel.

They think they rescued me, but they didn't. There are captive girls back there who need me. Especially Anna. What happens if she cries again?

I promised her and the other girls that I wouldn't abandon them. It was the first time I truly felt like a nun, comforting them.

All I want in life is to help others.

Now I feel as though I *have* abandoned them. I don't have much in this life, but I have my word.

These men don't care.

"I have to go back," I tell Tito yet again.

"Wait for Viktor," he says. "You can ask Viktor."

Cold comes over me. Viktor. The name on my chest. "Viktor?"

"The man who took you out of there."

"I will not wait. I will not stay." I make for the door.

He blocks it. "Not likely, sister." He points at a chair near the fireplace. "Sit."

I pull the ends of my head scarf tight under my chin and cross my arms, surveying the exits.

I want nothing to do with my old life. A life that gave me a body full of ugly scars.

"Fine, stand," he says.

Nikki sits instead, swinging an arm over the back of the chair. "Anyone got a smoke?"

"Act right and we'll see," Tito says.

I turn away from the strange familiarity of this scene. People like this, a place like this.

I don't want to know what I was.

Mother Olga always said that God can forgive even the worst of sinners if they come to him with the right feeling in their heart, but what if I was evil? What if I enjoyed killing people?

Ever since I saw that precious light coming from that icon in the thicket, my life has been a journey toward love.

I want so badly to be good.

Sometimes I feel that old life on the edges of my awareness, like a dangerous fog that might swallow up the goodness if I let it.

I reach into my pocket, close my fingers around a corner of the icon.

Tito has several other American men under his command—two inside here, more outside. This habit of counting men and assessing force, this too comes from that dark life. I do not want it.

They ask us whether we want lunch. Nikki wants a burger.

I'm not hungry.

Again Tito asks me to sit. I ask for a phone.

"I need you to sit."

I stand. It seems to make him nervous. I take up a pen and paper and write a phone number. It's the cellphone for the convent in Ukraine. "Please call and tell them I'm okay."

Tito takes it and pockets it.

Suddenly, the door opens and a burly bald man comes in with bags, looking excited. He addresses me in Russian—"It's really you!" He searches my eyes with a smile so huge and crooked it makes me feel fond of him. He can't believe I don't recognize him.

I nod politely. I don't know him.

He hands the bags to Tito, not taking his eyes from me. "Tanechka—remember me?—Mischa? C'mon, Tata…"

"I'm sorry. I'm not her. Please, bring me back to that place. If you think you're my friend, if you have any feeling for me, Mischa—bring me back."

Mischa looks torn, troubled. Tito shrugs.

"Blank slate, folks," Nikki says.

"Tanechka…" Mischa says again, then pauses, as though there's so much he wants to say.

"Viktor's on his way," Tito says.

Mischa unpacks the bags and arranges pastries on a plate—*vatrushkas* with curd cheese in the center and lemon wedges. He steals glances at me. "Viktor thought you might be hungry."

I shake my head.

"Yeah, well, you'll go sit at the table and eat the snack Mischa brought, or I'll tie you there," Tito says.

Mischa growls at Tito. "Be nice. She's ours."

Tito shrugs.

I sit, but I don't eat. Mischa stands by, a strong, silent presence, like a tree. "It's good to have you. So good," he says after a while.

Nikki eats everything in sight. Afterwards, she snatches a pack of cigarettes from the pocket of a nearby jacket and lights up. Tito slaps it right out of her mouth. "Not in Viktor's place."

She stands up and goes for him, and he simply pushes her back down.

She laughs at him. "Punk."

Nikki never wanted me to comfort her. She would be a lovely young woman if only she'd brush her dark hair out of her eyes and sit nicely. Instead she sits with one leg thrown over the arm of the couch. The men in that place dressed her in a short white frock and white knee socks, and sitting like that, her undergarments show.

"Nikki—your—" I gesture to convey my meaning.

She simply sneers. "Yeah, you can't get me out of these fucking clothes fast enough." She smirks over at Tito. Tito pretends not to notice, but he notices.

"There are women's clothes above," one of the guys says.

Tito shakes his head. "Everybody stays in a holding pattern here until Aleksio or Viktor gets back."

"Come on, Tito," Nikki says. "You like me in this getup? Yeah, I think you love me in this pervy getup."

Tito gets a dark look, then he tips up his chin. "Carlo, you take her up there and let her put something decent on. No messing shit up. Got it?"

The guard brings Nikki up.

I scan around the home, which has pleasing colors, a pleasing arrangement. I won't stay, though. "It is his?"

"Viktor's? Yes," Mischa says.

"I do not know him."

Mischa exchanges glances with Tito.

"And I will not stay."

Mischa just stares at me. You'd think I'm a talking rabbit, the way he stares. Then Nikki comes back down in jeans, sneakers, and a torn black T-shirt that shows her belly button. Mischa widens his eyes and watches me with renewed intensity.

"Metallica for the win." Nikki makes a hand signal of some sort, showing me two pointer fingers, two pinkies.

Mischa continues to watch me, as though I might react to Nikki in these new clothes. Why? I'm happy she has a new outfit. The old outfit was for the men, not for her.

Footfalls outside the door. I know it's that Viktor, the one who plucked me from that place. I know it before he enters.

The door flies open.

He pauses, framed in the doorway. He wears a black suit, tie askew. He's shed the stuffing that made him look large. His face is hard and square, but his chocolate-brown eyes sparkle. A little dent forms in his chin as he smiles.

He looks so happy, and somewhere deep down inside me, the thought that he's beautiful rises up.

"Tanechka."

"Please take me back, Viktor. You know where it is. Those girls need me."

Viktor closes the distance between us. He kneels down at my feet, clutching the thick fabric of my nun's robe, looking up at me from under inky lashes.

I don't know what to do with this man kneeling at my feet like this. It stirs emotions in me, like the air after a rainstorm—fresh and a little bit like tears.

"*Lisichka*," he says. Little fox.

Something tugs at the edges of my mind. I steel myself and address him in Russian. "I don't know you." I try to back up. He won't let me. "Take me back."

He presses his forehead to my thighs through the coarse dark material. I feel his heat, his electricity. "I'm so sorry, *lisichka*."

I push him off me—with more violence than I should—and he lands on the floor. "I'm not that one," I say urgently. "Return me."

"Tanechka," Nikki says. "Sister—whatever—I think you should reconsider, because this guy's pretty fine. IMHO."

"What the fuck do are you wearing?" Viktor barks at Nikki. "Those clothes belong to Tanechka."

"No, they don't," I say.

Viktor turns to me. "What's the last thing you remember?"

"The first thing, do you mean?"

A stormy look comes into his eyes. "Fine. First thing."

"If you won't let me go back, did you at least alert the police about what they're doing to the women there?"

"We're handling it, trust me." He stands. "Please, Tanechka, you won't even tell me that?"

Strange how I can feel his heart. There are so many things I know about this man. It feels like a wagon wheel finding the groove in the road.

"I was in a tree jutting out from one of the sheer faces of Dariali Gorge," I say.

"Tanechka." The way Viktor says my name is so full of emotion, I think he might burst into flames.

I hold up my hand. "I don't want to know about my old life. Or how I fell."

Viktor and Mischa exchange glances.

"If you're truly my friends, you'll be happy for me—happy that I found peace, happy that God sent me to the convent. And then to the brothel."

"God didn't send you—"

"God gave me a chance to start anew—"

Viktor's voice booms. "No more of this, Tanechka!"

I fold my arms. Something about him stirs me.

"I'm sorry," he whispers, bereft. "Forgive me."

My eyes go naturally to the pulse pounding madly in his throat, as if I knew to expect it there. I have the sense of his blood racing, a volcano trapped inside of him. I can feel his torment. He's the most tormented man I've ever seen.

Helplessly he studies my face.

I have the impulse to take him in my arms and whisper words of comfort against his cheek, to stop his suffering.

Another man bursts through the door, this one a thick-necked man with honey blond hair and a wide, frank face. In another life he could be an innocent country boy, but in this life he's a killer among killers. He was outside the virgin brothel when they took me. "Tanechka."

Viktor rests a hand on his shoulder. "Look—it's Yuri. Your good friend."

Yuri smiles wide and holds out his hands. "Oh, Tane-chka!"

I don't take his hands. I turn to Viktor. "I'd be so grateful if you would let me at least contact my convent…"

"Later."

"They're my family. They'll be worried about me."

Viktor says, "*We're* your family. I'm your family."

My heart pounds. "We were married?"

Viktor snorts, seeming almost angry. "We never had any use for papers or contracts. We were not the running dogs of the state bureaucracy. Our love was so strong, it transcended everything."

"I'm not her."

"You don't *know* that you're her, that's all."

"*You* don't know," I say.

Viktor closes his eyes and seems to center himself. He raises his hands. "It's okay." He speaks as if to calm me, but he's the one who needs calming. "You'll go at your pace."

"I'll go at no pace. I don't know you. That won't change."

More people come. Russian men who seem to know me, some other Americans, too.

Viktor comes to me, stands beside me. I feel shivers as his mouth nears my ear, his hand barely grazing my straight spine. "I want you to know you're safe now. You understand? You're safe with me. I won't let anything happen to you, and I'll never, ever hurt you."

"I want the girls freed," I say. "If you don't go and do that, I will."

"We're on it," Viktor says. "We'll take that organization down faster and more effectively than the cops ever could, okay?"

"When?"

"As soon as we can take it down in a way where they can't put it back up."

"Those girls can't wait."

"Trust me, we're on it," Viktor says, exasperated. He tells the people to leave us.

I stiffen. I don't want to be alone with this one.

An American steps forward and grabs Viktor by the shoulder. "You sure?"

"Yeah," Viktor says. "It's cool."

The man cups Viktor's cheek. His hair is longer than Viktor's, and curly, but otherwise he looks very much like Viktor. Same dark features, same bold noses, same generous lips.

This is his brother, it seems. An American brother.

Viktor smiles, but it isn't his real smile. It feels strange, the way I can read this Viktor.

Viktor's American brother makes a small hand motion. "Let's move it out." The group moves as one toward the door—all except for Nikki. Tito takes her by the arm.

"Leave her," I say to Tito. "If she doesn't want to go with you—"

Nikki snorts and shakes him off. "I got this, sister." She eyes Tito. "Can I have a smoke?"

Tito frowns. "Outside."

Nikki follows him out.

"You were always so protective," Viktor says.

Viktor's American brother stops in the doorway and turns. "We're coming back for dinner," he says. "We'll bring stroganoff and *pirozhki*. Okay?"

"Tanechka doesn't like potato *pirozhki*," Viktor says.

"Not true." I put my hand to my chest. "I like potatoes..."

"You don't like potato *pirozhki*, though, trust me. You always say it's the scam of the *pirozhki* world." He turns to his brother. "No potato *pirozhki*."

"Okay, man," the brother says.

And like that we're alone. In Russian, he says, "You don't like it. I'm saving you the trouble."

"I'm not her."

"I'm going to light a fire," Viktor says. "Don't try to leave. You won't get far."

I nod.

"I don't have to tell you that, do I? You probably marked exactly how many guys were out there when you came in. You always track your environment like that. You knew the camera was there in that room—I could tell. You notice and avoid cameras as easily as a fish swims."

It feels strange that he knows. He wads up a handful of paper and shoves it under a log in the fireplace. "We have to get you out of that stupid outfit."

My pulse races. "It's not stupid."

He stills, seeming to bite back hard words. Softly, he says, "You're not a nun."

"I'm a novice, hoping to be a nun. I wish you would contact my sisters in the monastery and tell them that I'm all right. It's near Donetsk."

He turns. "You got all the way to Donetsk?"

"The countryside, in Donetsk Oblast. Not the city."

He asks so many questions, I end up telling the story—the short version, anyway. The hospital. Meeting Mother Olga. Nothing of the icon. I don't want to hear him mocking my experience with the icon.

"You must have been so frightened."

"I was," I say. "I was mostly thirsty, and in so much pain."

"Tanechka—"

I hold up a hand. I don't want his pity or his passion. All of his emotions are too large. "I don't want to talk about it. Okay?"

"How about you change into your normal clothes. I have clothes for you."

"No thanks."

He turns away and sets a smaller log on top, concentrating fiercely. "You never did take shit from anyone."

"Stop speaking as though you know me. You knew me once, but you don't know me now."

He turns. "*You* don't know you, that's the problem." He shoves at the logs and then flicks a long match. Some paper catches. The light kisses his cheekbones, causes his short inky hair to glow brown. He shoves in a poker, and the fire roars to life. It's nice. "*You* don't know *you*," he says again.

The flames dance, lighting the room. It is all the cozier for the gray day outside. I draw near.

"You used to love fires," he says.

I sniff. It seems everything I do stokes his hope like the fire warming the room.

"We'd speak in English like this. Always English to practice. We had the best English skills of all our gang."

That explains some things. "The English I still remember."

"When I saw you on the website, Tanechka, you can't imagine." The fire burns brightly behind him now, lighting the edges of him. "Everything stopped for me when...you were gone. And then seeing you again—I couldn't believe it. You'd never turn to the camera, of course, but I knew it was you—just like you know me. You can't fool me. You're confused, but I think your heart knows me."

"Viktor," I say, his name a familiar shape on my lips. "I can't be who you want."

"You're *always* who I want." He looks around. "I was going to rent some crash pad, but when I saw you, saw we had this chance, I vowed to do this right. Make this beautiful home... Do you recognize any of this furniture? I had this chair sent over from Moscow. That's where you're from." He moves to a gold chair with a carved wood frame. "You remember it?"

The hope in his eyes is so intense, it breaks my heart a little bit. "I do not."

"We got it at that flea market in Omsk. And the spring inside? I always said to throw it away because the spring made it uncomfortable to sit on, and guests would complain, but you loved this thing. You said, 'It's one little piece of wire!'"

Dimples deepen on his cheeks as he smiles at the memory. The dimples do something strange to my belly.

"You said, 'One little piece of wire won't get the best of me.'" He looks so happy. Talking about the chair makes him live in that other time.

He kneels in front of the chair, running his hand over part of the cushion, then he looks up at me, face raw with hope. "You can still see the place where you ripped up the cushion so you could get under there and fix it. Come. Look."

I stay where I am.

"You never gave up on anything. You hated quitters. Oh, you really hated quitters." The smile fades. "Just come and look. You couldn't get the exact right color of thread."

I sit on the couch. "Enough."

He shuts his eyes. It's what he does when he tries to quell his emotions.

"I get it—this is all going too fast for you. You had a trauma. You have amnesia. I'm going to help you, though. It's okay if you don't remember everything. Maybe it's even better to not remember everything at once."

I sigh, trying not to enjoy the fire.

He comes to me then, sits right next to me. I feel him on my skin, in my belly. "Do you truly not want to remember?"

"I told you what I want. I want to contact the convent. I want to know what you're doing for my captive sisters, and if you aren't planning on freeing them immediately, I want you to set me free so I can go back there myself. Maybe I'll bring the police and we'll free them."

"Right, the police. How will you know which of them you can trust? Do you think a place like that can run without police protection? We have it under control. I was there planting surveillance and getting into their network. It's being handled."

I gaze at the fire, hating this helplessness.

"You say you don't want to know your old life, but how do you know which is the better life if you don't know anything about one of them?" He takes my hand. My fingers spark at his touch. "You don't know."

"I know what I have now is better than any other possible life."

"The life that you had before, it was glorious."

"Is that why my body's covered with scars? My body is proof that the life I had wasn't glorious."

"The life, maybe not always, but *you* were glorious. You were a warrior. Fierce and so beautiful and brave. You were..." He trails off, searching for words. He's beautiful when he remembers her. "You shone," he finally says. "Brighter than anything—"

"Some things shine brighter."

"Wrong. You were so impressive, brave..." His sadness is a raw thing. "You were my whole heart." He takes my hands and presses his forehead to the unruly ball that our hands make together.

My blood thunders.

"I need you to remember." He lifts his brown eyes once again to me. "You saw the tattoo. Could that lie?"

"It was a different life," I say gently. "People change."

He studies my eyes as if to search for the woman he lost, but he's the one who's lost. He's lost and beautiful. I stare at our fingers together, mesmerized by his warmth, by the rough familiarity of his skin.

"I never thought I'd touch you again, never imagined..." He kisses my fingers, quick, fervent kisses that swell something inside me, as if his kisses are nourishment. He glances up at me, then he turns his face back down and kisses my fingers again, and this time his kisses are slow, his lips warm and soft. A strange and pleasant feeling spreads all through me.

Lust.

I yank my hands from his.

I was drugged, kidnapped, threatened, kept prisoner in an underground brothel. I was forced to eat meals with a sick and twisted man, but I was never truly frightened.

Until now.

"I am *not* her. Respect that."

His look is stern and dark. He stands. "I respect Tanechka. Tanechka would want me to fight for her. She'd do the same for me."

"I *am* Tanechka. I'm the new Tanechka."

CHAPTER EIGHT

Viktor

Tanechka stops talking with me an hour after she arrives.

I tell her that there are clothes in the drawers and the closet. She informs me again that she won't change, and she closes the door and locks it.

Fine. The bedroom is a nice room. She'll be surrounded by familiar things.

Aleksio and Mira come by before dinnertime.

"Anything on Kiro?" I need some good news. I need to know he's not locked away in a prison where we can't get to him.

Aleksio shakes his head. "Nada."

I suck in a breath. "Okay, then."

"Nice. I didn't know you had this in you," Mira says, fingering the rich red tablecloth, embroidered with folk art designs.

"It's Tanechka. This is like the home she made for us in Moscow."

"She still doesn't…" Mira begins.

I shrug. "She doesn't remember. *Yet*. It says online to surround her with familiar things. Familiar people."

"What if she still can't remember?"

"She will."

Aleksio studies my face. "What if she *does* remember? Isn't that dangerous?"

"Whatever happens, I just want her back."

He looks away. "The good news is that your frame worked. Out at Valhalla. They don't suspect you were anyone."

We focus on Valhalla, going over what our tech guys have gleaned from their computer files so far. They've identified pipelines and intermediaries. Aleksio shows me a chart he has begun. Like something the police might make.

Yuri, Tito, and Nikki arrive along with the rich scent of stroganoff, followed soon after by Pityr, Mischa, and a few others. We set out the feast.

Yuri admires the rich red tablecloth, embroidered with black folk designs. "So Tanechka."

Aleksio sets the ten-serving to-go pan onto the table. I make him use the serving dish. Tanechka always wanted to use proper dishes.

Aleksio regards me strangely. "Whatever, brother."

"Tanechka liked things nice," I say to Mira. "She came up poor. but she wouldn't be pushed down by it. Even once we were rich in the Bratva, she would insist on nice dishes. Table manners."

"She would get so angry when one of us would throw a plate," Yuri says. "Though she was the one to throw them half the time."

"You Russians are so fucking dramatic," Aleksio says. "Is she up there?"

"Yes. Locked herself in the bedroom." I set out the candles and light them. "She'll come." I serve our guests vodka, belt back one of my own.

"A nun," Mischa says. "She never did anything halfway, that's for sure."

"Remember her wildcat stare?" Yuri says.

I laugh.

"*Blyad*," Mischa says. "That stare. That temper."

Yuri turns to Aleksio and Mira. "Her stare of hate could cut a man in half. She would line her eyes in black makeup, and they would be like two lasers burning at you. When you were on her good side, there was nothing she wouldn't do for you, but get on her bad side..."

"It starts with the stare. Ends in blood," Mischa says, exchanging glances with Yuri.

"What?" I demand.

"Do you have a plan for when she remembers you killed her?" Yuri asks.

"I'll wing it."

"Wing it?" Yuri bites out. "You don't wing it with Tanechka. She's a 'rip out your intestines, ask questions later' girl."

"You don't want her armed when she remembers," Mischa says.

"You think I don't know how to manage Tanechka?" I leave the table and go upstairs to get her.

Tanechka doesn't stir when I knock at the door.

"Tanechka," I say. "It's dinnertime. Do I need to break down the door?"

She comes and flings it open. She still wears the severe black robe, buttoned up to the neck, and the black scarf tied around her chin.

Behind her I see that she has cleared off a bookshelf and placed the icon of Jesus on a cloth on one of the low shelves. I cringe to think of her praying to it. Kissing the feet of Jesus.

"Dinner," I say.

She just stares at me with those deep blue eyes. Wary, but hungry, I think.

"I know you're already planning your escape. You'll need food, right?"

"Fine."

Everybody stands when I lead her in. Tanechka is gorgeous in the candlelight, and the wisps of blond hair that sneak out from her scarf glow like white gold. She greets her old *bratki* politely but without recognition.

Tanechka. It feels dangerous to hope. Still I hope with every fiber of myself. I pour her a vodka.

"Thank you, no," she says. "Water, please."

Nikki rolls her eyes.

Water with dinner is not her way, but I pour her a water. My Tanechka does not like to be told what to do. She asks Nikki if she's contacted her family.

"Yeah, I'm good as is," Nikki says.

Back in Russia we loved to have wild dinner parties. Now Tanechka wears a nun's robe and head scarf to dinner.

She's here at least. The men start to eat.

"Aren't we going to give thanks?" she asks.

"No," I say.

I pass Mira's plate, find her glaring at me. She thinks I should play along? Hell, no.

Tanechka gives thanks on her own, silently, head bowed.

Her prayer grates on me. The article on amnesia I read said to surround her with familiarity, and prayer is not a familiar part of our old life.

Guns and booze and fucking. That's our old life. That's what I'll surround her with. As soon as we fuck, she'll have her memories back. I'm sure of it.

We eat. I turn the conversation to Sky World, a rundown amusement park outside Moscow we used to go to as kids. Tanechka does not remember it.

Yuri has the party laughing with his descriptions of the wooden roller coaster, and then the swinging platform ride. The rides at Sky World, they were so dangerous. Even Tanechka smiles. Her smile fills me with so much happiness it nearly spills over into tears.

The rides are especially shocking to Aleksio, Mira, Nikki, and Tito—this is part of what makes it funny.

"You Americans," Yuri snarls. "With your smooth plastic playgrounds like easy chairs." We argue about this, but Tanechka doesn't seem amused anymore. The silent treatment.

Mira asks her questions now and then about her life in the convent, and Tanechka answers politely. Always a short answer. Yes or no, if possible. She thinks we're no better than the brothel, but I saw her laugh. The old Tanechka peeking through. I'll have her back.

The one time she speaks up, it's about the brothel yet again.

"You should have left me and taken the girls. I would've been fine." She waves her hand, taking in the table. "All of this. I'm grateful, but I don't need it. I could've endured what those women couldn't."

I throw back a glass of vodka, welcoming the clean, hard burn. "We will rescue the women."

Aleksio explains about the police being compromised. That it would be shut down temporarily or maybe moved if we don't strike deep into the network. "Think of it as a ceiling," he says to her. "Just closing this brothel is like fixing a leak in the ceiling by painting over the stain."

"You tell it to the virgin there awaiting the man who bought her. Frightened, alone. What would she say about your *ceiling*?"

I bite back a smile. She's glorious.

Aleksio explains the big picture to her more carefully, as if she didn't understand the first time.

Tanechka understood fine. She's annoyed, impatient. I exchange amused glances with Yuri—we're both seeing it.

"Your explanations mean nothing to me," she spits. "A lot of talk and no action."

Mischa bites his lip. Pityr beams. Tanechka doesn't understand why it can't be stopped *now*. She sees girls in trouble. Go, take them out. That's her attitude. Fuck everything. *So Tanechka.*

I set down my glass. "Would you have us shutting it down in a violent way, then? Would you like that instead?"

"A false choice," she says. "There are more options than those two."

"Maybe pray?" I challenge.

"You tell the police and trust in that. You find the good ones and tell them."

"Please!" A comment like that is beyond childish. Tanechka would never say it.

"The police are there for a reason," she says.

"The police are for rent in this town," I say. "Haven't you been listening? It's not so different in Russia. You just don't remember."

She gives me a challenging look. She'll have none of my shit. It warms my heart.

She turns to Mira at one point. She's rightly identified her as a possible ally. "Surely there's an Orthodox church here in Chicago."

"You're not going to a fucking church," I say.

"They'd let me contact my sisters in the convent."

"So will I," I say. "As soon as you change out of that nun costume."

"It's not a costume."

An awkward silence falls over the table. Yuri tries with more stories of Sky World, but the fun is lost.

Later in the kitchen Mira scolds me, tells me that this is a horrible choice I've left Tanechka with.

I shrug. "It's done."

"What if I call her convent?" she says. "You said she couldn't, but I could."

"If she cares about talking to her sisters there, she'll change out of her nun clothes."

"You're acting like a jackass. Why would she even want to remember anything if you're the guy she'd end up with?"

I grab the box from Petrovsky's and begin to arrange the *orehi* on a colorful plate.

"What are those?"

"Nuts, we call them. *Orehi.* Cookie dough with brown custard inside. A silly child's treat, but Tanechka loved them."

"She won't give in on the clothes now."

"I know. So stubborn." I know it better than Mira.

"So stop trying to make her change by taking things away from her," she says. "Why not *give* her things she loves instead?"

"What do you think I'm doing?" I press my fists to the cool marble counter. "What is this dinner? This whole place?"

"She didn't choose this, *you* did. If you give a little, maybe she'll give a little."

"This is the lawyer talking?" Mira's a lawyer, starting a new practice in Chicago these days. She loves the law. Not so convenient for Aleksio, but their love is strong.

"No, it's your friend talking, telling you not to be an asshole. Think about letting me call her people at least. Tito says she gave him the number. He probably has it in his pocket. I could call and let them know she's okay."

I say nothing.

"Maybe letting those sisters know she's okay will help her see that you're not so bad."

She has a point. "Okay, do it. I'll send in Tito. And Mischa in case you need translation."

"Good man."

I storm out feeling angry and upset. "Dessert," I say, setting down the plate in the waning candlelight. I tell Tito and Mischa that Mira wants them.

Yuri and Pityr are excited. We didn't so much love *orehi*—far too sweet for us—but we used to tease Tanechka about it. We start passing around the plate. Everybody takes one or two. I set three on the small side plate in front of Tanechka.

"Are these Petrovsky's?" Pityr asks.

"Yes," I say. All of us fight not to stare at Tanechka. She doesn't recognize the orehi, though. This I can see.

Mira and Mischa come out a few minutes later. Mira announces she called Tanechka's convent.

Tanechka stands, stunned. "Will you let me speak to them?"

"I hung up, but Mother Olga has a message for you. They're all healthy and well, and something about a rooster looking forward to seeing you."

Tanechka tears up. "*Petushik*," she whispers. "What else?"

"They're happy to hear you're okay, Tanechka. They were worried."

Mischa nods. "They sounded good."

"What about the fighting on the border? The attacks—there was an old guard, and he was not so strong. You're sure they're okay?"

"All okay. They said for you not to worry."

"Did you tell them I want to talk to them? That I'm trying?"

Mira casts a glance at me, the ogre. "I told them that you wanted badly to talk to them and that you would, soon."

"Thank you."

I shove an *orehi* into my mouth.

What kind of man am I? I couldn't have shown this one small kindness to the woman I love?

I close my eyes, and I'm back at the edge of Dariali Gorge with her clinging onto me, the vast space below.

Predatel! I call her. Reminding myself why I must kill her. She betrayed the Bratva. A traitor.

Even as she falls, she reaches for me, terror and disbelief in her eyes. Her face is burned into my mind, into my dreams.

The talk rumbles on, but I've had too much to drink. I feel like weeping.

I watch the candlelight waver on the thick red tablecloth, feeling hopeless. Hating myself for what I did to her.

"So delicious," Tanechka says.

I look up to see her staring at her empty plate. Her gaze lights on the plate with the rest of the *orehi*. "Delicious."

"Would you like more?

She looks down. She wants more. Desperately. But she shakes her head. "No," she says softly. "Gluttony."

CHAPTER NINE

Aleksio

I let Tanechka have our bedroom—alone. I sleep in a guest bedroom, or at least I try to.

She comes down in the morning neat as a pin, still in her nun's dress and head scarf. I leave her to herself, giving her space.

She asks again to search for a Russian Orthodox church in town.

Again I say no.

She regards me with her burning gaze. My heart leaps. That's the old Tanechka poking through.

I decide we'll go on a picnic. We used to picnic in a park near a lake, and she liked it. Lake Michigan is larger and windier, but I think she'll enjoy it.

First I need to buy the perfect supplies. I talk to Sander, one of our new guys, who's stationed outside the door. We have plenty of money to hire new muscle like Sander. If they prove their loyalty, they'll have a hand in the business our father built—once we take it back from Bloody Lazarus.

"Keep her in there while I'm gone. Don't let that nun costume fool you," I tell Sander. "She's every inch a killer under there."

He nods. He understands, or at least he thinks he does. Nobody truly understands Tanechka.

I start off down the sidewalk. This is the old part of town, lined with brownstones. The trees blaze with yellow leaves. A block away, I turn back, go back to Sander.

"Four men around this perimeter still?" I ask him. He nods. "Find another and make it five. She's going to try to leave, and I don't want her hurt."

I instruct Mischa and Yuri to tell the Americans how good she is at escapes. Mischa insists they have it under control. "Tell them," I say. "They need to hear it from you, too."

When I return, I find none of the men out there. I burst into the house, and there they are, all in the living room. Tanechka's sitting on the floor, cuffed to a radiator pipe.

I growl.

"She's okay," Mischa says.

I kneel next to her. "You're okay?"

"Aside from needing to leave?" She yanks on her cuff. I love her so much I can't think.

I step outside with Mischa, who fills me in. It seems she tried to get out as soon as I was around the block. The group of them grabbed her. "Very gently," he assures me.

Ona nasha dorogaya podruga, he calls her—"the one we love the most."

I thank him and send them back out, then I unlock Tanechka. "If you have to pee, go now. We're leaving for a picnic."

She rubs her wrist, glaring at me.

An hour later we're parking on the lakefront. It's a sunny, brilliant fall day, the sky electric blue—candy sky, she used to call it. I've brought her a sweater, but she doesn't want it. Nuns back home are famously ascetic.

No matter. I get out, grab the picnic basket and blanket, and go around to her door.

She looks up at me warily.

It is all I can do to stop myself from taking her cheeks and kissing her.

She doesn't wish to get out.

"You want me to carry you?"

This gets her out. I give her the sweater and lead her across the pale, cool sand toward the dark water, rough with whitecaps. The beach is deserted today. People aren't so interested in the beach in autumn. Always everything needs to be perfect for the Americans.

She gives me one of her challenging Tanechka looks. Just this look fills my heart with love. She addresses me in Russian. "Aren't you worried I'll try to run off?"

"Maybe I'd like it. Maybe I'd enjoy catching you."

Quickly she looks away. Sander and his men tailed us, just in case. You never want to underestimate Tanechka.

I turn and walk backwards. "This isn't your first time in America. Did you know that? Twice we were here."

"In Chicago?"

"No. Once in Omaha, once in San Francisco. You liked the old houses in San Francisco. You said they looked like frosted cookies."

"Hmmph." She looks away as she so often does when I remind her of our old life. I tell myself it's a good sign that she runs from these memories. You only run from something if it's a threat.

"You said you wanted to eat those houses right up." Both times we traveled to America it was to chase and kill those who betrayed the Bratva, but I don't say that. Omaha got quite bloody. We had to kill one person extra before it was over.

"We were put together because we both knew English. I was born here. You didn't know that—neither did I, until a year ago."

She simply watches me.

"I was born here in Chicago to an Albanian family. I was two years old, just learning to talk, when the man my father trusted most attacked our family. Our father ran a business dynasty that stretched across the entire middle of the nation. But this man—Mira's father—he drugged our parents and killed them."

"Mira? The one Aleksio loves?"

"Yes. Her father and a man called Bloody Lazarus destroyed our family. They drugged our parents and chased them up to the nursery where my brothers and I were. My parents wanted to protect us. Instead they were slaughtered in front of us."

"You saw it?"

"I remember only...impressions. Aleksio saw it all, in the reflection of a window. He was nine."

Her gaze goes tender. "I'm sorry."

"This old hit man, Konstantin, a veteran of the Kosovo wars, he held Aleksio in the shadows, hand over his mouth so he wouldn't scream. Konstantin saved Aleksio's life. Our enemies sold me and Kiro, our baby brother, but they would have killed Aleksio. They tried to. All his life, killers were after Aleksio. Me, they sent me across the world to that orphanage in Moscow with no identification. They sold our *bratik* Kiro into an adoption ring. We still can't find him."

Her look of tenderness means everything.

"Bloody Lazarus wants to kill Kiro. He doesn't want us three brothers to be together. We're doing everything we can to find Kiro first."

"Do you think you will?"

I turn and walk by her side. "I hope so. Aleksio's sure we can, but every lead we have comes up to nothing. Lazarus is really powerful, and Kiro is probably locked up somewhere, totally vulnerable."

"You're scared," she observes. "Because you love your little brother."

"Yes," I whisper. "I try to be upbeat for Aleksio, but you don't know Lazarus. Lately I've felt like we've doomed him."

"It's okay to be scared," she says, "but there's always hope." She takes my hand. "Look inside yourself and you can find it."

I swallow. She took my hand.

"You came back," I say.

She lets go. "I was talking about Kiro."

We continue in silence.

"You don't seem American."

"I was taken at the ago of two. You thought I was so smart, the way I could think and even dream in English. It's because the language was inside me from that time. I didn't remember, but the pathways in my brain had been created for English. Because I was a little boy here."

"Mmm," she says.

Again I turn and walk backwards. I like to watch her face. "Do you want to know how you came to learn English?"

Behind her the trees in their fall colors. Gleaming hotels and skyscrapers soar above Lake Shore Drive.

"You don't want to know?"

"It's immaterial."

I stop when I decide we're at the perfect spot. I spread out the blanket. I sit and open the basket. "Sit."

"Do I have a choice?"

"You prefer to stand?"

She sits stiffly, like the nun she wants me to take her for, but a small, bright lock of hair has broken free from under her scarf, flying and waving at me like a small flag. I wonder how long her hair is under there. She used to keep it long—she said it gave her a greater diversity of styles. A good killer is a good chameleon.

"You learned English easily because of your obsession with rock and roll," I say. "That's how you came to know it. Memorizing songs."

She frowns.

I take out the bottles of sparkling lemon water, unscrew the top of one, and set it down on a platter. She loves anything citrus. Flavors with bite. Everything with an edge, even sex. She liked to be held tight, to be held down. *Make me know you're there,* she'd whisper. *Make me know, Viktor.*

That was code for her wanting me to be more forceful. She loved to fuck.

I remove a small box from the basket and open it, pleased to see that the honey cake survived the trip. I place a piece on a small painted plate and set it in front of her next to her fizzy lemon water. She used to enjoy such water with vodka.

She thanks me politely. "*Spasibo.*"

"*Nezashto.*" I take out the book, the poems of Anatoly Vartov.

"A book," she says.

I grit my teeth. *A book.* This isn't just *a book;* it's her favorite collection of poems in the world. She had a fiercely personal relationship with each and every one of them, especially the poem titled "Cages." There was a dark time in her life when she would read it and cry for the beauty of it. Like a gift to her, this poem. "I thought we would read." I stretch out on my back. "I could read to you if you like."

"It won't work, Viktor. You won't make me remember."

"Then what's the harm?"

She sighs, seeming to relax, and I think maybe Mira was right. You can't force a flower to bloom, but you can show it the sun.

Tanechka eyes her honey cake. "I require only simple food."

"Honey cake isn't so complicated."

She bites into her cake and chews without expression, as if it's cardboard. It was one of her favorites—layers of honey-soaked cake with creamy frosting between each one. A girl's cake. She pauses, still looking at nothing, but there's a slight light in her eyes. She likes it.

My heart feels like it might explode.

Her famous focus was good for more than killing; it allowed her to enjoy beauty and pleasure more deeply than other people.

I want to tell her this is something that I loved about her very much, but I hold back. I want this moment to be for her, not for me.

She casts her gaze down at the cake. "Not bad," she says softly.

I look away before she can catch the shine in my eyes.

I'd give her anything if only she'd come back. I'd give her a blade and tell her to cut my throat.

Out the corner of my eye I see her take another bite. I school my features to look unimpressed.

"Usually it's the Russian babies going to the West."

"Yes," I say.

"Why did he do it?"

I try not to show too much happiness that she's engaged me. "My father lifted Mira's father up to make him his right-hand man, but it wasn't enough. He wanted the power that our father possessed. My brothers and I were obstacles. Mira's father is dead now, but his dangerous *kumar*, Lazarus, is even worse. Lazarus is the man who owns Valhalla, where you were. There was a prophecy—"

"I don't believe in prophecies."

"I don't either, but a lot of people do, and that's what gives them power. An old crone, honored for her predictions, pointed to the three of us brothers at a party soon after Kiro was born. She said that we brothers together were unbeatable. 'You boys. Together you rule...you boys, you three boys.' Aleksio thinks it was part of why Lazarus and Mira's father went after us."

Out the corner of my eye I catch her focusing on the box where the rest of the cake still waits. Two more pieces.

I try not to smile. "There's more."

"I do not think I want it."

I wave my hand. "Feed it to the gulls, then."

She folds her hands in her lap. Oh, she wants the cake. "Your enemies want to keep you from reuniting?"

The old Tanechka would not ask such an obvious question.

"Yes," I say.

"Lazarus believes in the prophecy?"

"Probably not. But within...our community, it would be a huge psychological advantage for him to kill Kiro. People will more readily follow him. It's not so easy to kill me or Aleksio. But Kiro is out there lost."

I sit up and put another piece on her plate, then I gaze out at a distant freighter, allowing her privacy. She very much wants that cake.

I tell her about Kiro, how he might be a wild boy. I tell her about the joy I felt when Aleksio showed up at a garage in Moscow. Tanechka would have been every bit as happy for me as Yuri was, seeing that I had a brother. She would've jumped into my arms, and the three of us would have gone out and torn up the town.

Now she just listens.

She reaches out and pulls a bit of spongy cake from the edge. My heart lifts. But then she throws it. Gulls fly over. One takes it and flies off. She throws out the rest, bit by bit, feeding the gulls.

So Tanechka. She will not be managed.

CHAPTER TEN

Tanechka

T he gulls finally leave. I lie back, gazing at the sky. "Such a beautiful blue."

He says nothing. I can't tell whether he's happy or sad. So often he seems to have both emotions flowing through him. Never have I met a man so volatile.

Then again, I have not met so many men.

That I remember, anyway.

He stares at the lake, arms planted behind him, sleeves rolled up to reveal forearms wild with sinew and muscle.

Thick, thick fingers spread out on the picnic blanket.

I enjoy looking at his fingers. I know I shouldn't.

If he is to be believed, he once touched me everywhere with those fingers. I can't imagine what it would be like, to allow him to touch me with those thick fingers.

Sometimes his gaze is so strong, seeing too much. Did he gaze like that upon my naked body?

He turns to me. "What are you thinking, Tanechka?"

"Many things."

"I wish I could take all of the pain you felt in that gorge. I would die ten times over to spare you from it. I would do anything—"

"I wouldn't want you to take it away. What happened was a gift," I say.

He grits his teeth and looks away. He doesn't agree that it was a gift.

He has four guards following us. He thinks I don't know. I saw two when we got out of the car. Two more later. Three are on the road behind us. One lingers near the shuttered snack stand some distance away.

Perhaps he's right to have four on me. I sometimes get ideas about escaping, seemingly out of nowhere, like a hidden helper passing me a note. I often picture the floor plan of the home he has me trapped in as a diagram in my mind. The idea of the roof has come to me several times. The row of homes is so tightly packed, the roof will be like a highway. This way of thinking feels like a well-worn path.

He wants to read the poetry to me.

I tell him no.

I don't like the way he knows things about me. Like the honey cake. The *orehi*. The fizzy water. I love these things too much. It's not fair that he knows. I love looking at his fingers. What would Mother Olga say?

He wants to play music, then, but I will not have it—not after what he told me about my love of American rock and roll.

I'm afraid to love these things. Like I'll forget about being a nun. Forget about the girls back in Valhalla. He says they're on it, but I feel so impatient.

He reaches into the basket and pulls out a block with squares of color on it. He hands it to me, and instinctively I begin to turn the parts this way and that, knowing it is wrong and that it must be made right.

"Rubik's Cube," he says. "We used to love them. We would race."

I pause. Another trick. I want to finish it. Red squares are where blues should be. The green, the red. It pains me not to finish it.

"Go on."

I set it aside. "Another life."

He picks it up. "What can it hurt?"

I try to resist, but I can't. I grab it and finish it in five twists, then I toss it aside, trying to blot out the feeling of triumph.

He lies down next to me now, on his belly, head propped in his hands, grinning. "Don't you want to know how you know how to do that?"

"No," I say. I can't let him know how badly I want to do it again.

"You used to be curious as a cat. It would sometimes get you into trouble."

His nearness gives me an unruly feeling. I should sit up, let the feeling shake out of me. But such a sudden movement would reveal too much.

So I stay. I pretend to be unaffected by him.

"You always loved stories and mysteries." He takes hold of a bit of fabric from my sleeve and rubs it between his thumb and forefinger—unconsciously, it seems. But nothing this man does is unconscious. Best to remember.

"I remember once we had a ring that somebody lost—a ruby ring with an unusual pattern. Celtic, you thought."

He doesn't touch my skin, only my sleeve. Still, he has a gravitational pull.

He continues to speak. The velvet of his voice sweeps against my skin.

He's too good. He's too *everything*, just like the honey cake.

"You called on scholars to identify the unusual design, then you researched designers and stores. You had endless ideas for finding the owner." He goes on, praising my resourcefulness.

I remove my sleeve from his grasp. I pretend to study the clouds.

It doesn't matter that we aren't touching. He still overwhelms my senses. "What happened?"

"We found the person."

"From just a ring?"

"Yes. Nobody thought we could do it, but you were tenacious. You and I found her house, just from the ring."

Something tugs at the corners of my mind. "Was she happy to have it back?"

A pause. "Who wouldn't be?"

The sun comes out from behind a passing cloud, and I close my eyes, basking in its warmth, basking a little bit also in his admiration.

That's when I feel him touch my cheek. Something inside me sparkles to life.

I turn and scowl.

He withdraws his hand. "You're not doing it right," he says. "You have to keep your eyes shut."

"What?"

"Come on. It's a game we used to play." He pushes my chin, turns my face back to the sky. "Close your eyes."

A bolt of pleasure shoots through me. My blood races. Everything feels dangerous and good.

"Close them. Do this one thing for me."

"Fine." I close my eyes. Again he touches my cheek—so lightly I almost can't feel it. Unbidden, my lips curl in a smile. I don't remember this game, but I remember the happy, pure feeling of it. The excitement of it.

"*Pomnish?*" he whispers. "Remember?"

"It's no use, Viktor."

"Keep your eyes closed," he says.

I feel his fingertips graze my cheek once again.

"*Pomnish?*"

I smile again because I know he'll kiss me there—I *need* for him to kiss me there just as day follows night.

Then I still. This is the game—touch the place you're going to kiss.

I should stop the game, but every molecule in me is waiting for his kiss, craving his kiss on my cheek, as if I need to finish this thing we have started.

It's as if he's communicating with my body, bypassing my mind completely. Is this what it's like to be hypnotized?

I feel him near.

My breath speeds as soft lips press to my cheek, lightly, quickly, then gone. I open my eyes.

He pulls away with the strangest look—a mixture of grief and joy. "You remember."

I don't remember, but my body does.

His gaze falls to my lips. He lifts his finger. He wants to do the game again, but I'm too fast—I grab his finger, bend it, threatening to break it. I know four ways to break this finger, and they array in my mind in order of pain. I squeeze, feeling the delineation of bones, horrified at the knowledge inside me.

Now he just looks happy. "You're remembering."

'What happened after she got the ring back? What's the rest of the story?"

He breaks eye contact.

I squeeze his finger. "Tell me the rest."

"Will you break my finger, Tanechka? Do you feel it? Just a twist."

"Tell me."

"Or you could break it at the middle joint."

I push away his hand. "You say you want me to remember. Then tell me the rest."

"You found the owner. She was happy to get it back."

"There's more."

"Do I look like a psychic? I can't predict people's futures."

"The woman who owned it—is she…okay?"

He gets a helpless look.

Everything in me clenches like a fist. "Tell me the rest."

"Tanechka," he whispers.

"Did I hurt her?"

He doesn't answer.

"Please," I beg. "Please tell me."

His look tells me everything.

I hurt her. Maybe killed her.

A seasick wave rolls through my belly. My voice is gravelly, as though dredged up from the rocky depths. "You wanted me to remember. *Tell me.*"

"You won't understand."

My throat feels so thick, I can barely get the words out. "I killed her. In cold blood."

"Tanechka."

"Get away from me!" I spring up and begin to run, feet sinking into the soft sand, frantic, pumping my arms, trying to go faster, faster, to outrun everything. I hear him panting behind me. He grabs me from behind and I plant myself, use his momentum to throw him over my shoulder. He lands on his back.

I pivot and run the other way, sand spraying.

Again he comes after me and this time he tackles me, bringing us both down. He rolls, taking the impact with his big body, holding me tightly.

I gasp for my breath as he flips us, him over me now.

"I killed her."

The weight of him presses me down. The soft sand is cool and rough on my cheek. "Shhh," he says, "you're okay."

"I'm not *okay*."

"You just need to remember who you are. You need to be yourself again."

"I'd rather die."

He holds me tight, crushing me with the violence of his emotion. "I won't let you die. Not again."

"I killed a person in cold blood." The knowledge is a wound. There's something warm in my chest, growing so fast I think it might break my ribs. I'm gasping for air, and suddenly the thing in me breaks and I'm sobbing—huge, heaving sobs.

He holds me, strokes my hair. "Shh."

"How can God forgive a person like me?"

"Tanechka." He strokes my hair.

I try to push him away, but he won't let go. I sob in his hateful arms. "I'm unforgivable."

"Never, *lisichka*. You're brave. You're beautiful."

I sob quietly, bereft.

He gasps his words into my hair, clutching me to his breast. "I would die for you a million times."

"No. It's right that I suffer. I was a killer. It is right that I should know the sweetness of God's love only to have it taken from me."

"Stop with the God stuff! Forget God! God forgot *you*. He abandoned you to hell before you could even walk. God doesn't deserve you."

"Get away from me!" I push him off. I don't run this time; I walk back to the car. He'll take me back to the flat. At least there I can be alone. I run my fingers over the familiar shape of my prayer rope, knot to knot, to the tassel at the end, representing the glory of the heavenly kingdom. He comes up beside me after a few minutes with our picnic basket.

"She was an assassin, you know. The woman you tracked through the ring. You saved lives by killing her."

"It's not for me to punish her." I stand by the car. He'll take me back to the flat. I'll bide my time. As soon as I'm able, I'll get away from this man. I'll save the girls. Then I'll go home.

"She was a killer," he says.

"You understand nothing." I practically spit out the words.

"I understand you have a beautiful heart."

CHAPTER ELEVEN

Lazarus

Tip of the day: When faking empathy, less is more.
A frown and a simple sentence, that's all you need.
At funerals, for example. The grieving wife or something.
I'm so sorry for your loss. So sorry. Even if you laughed as
you put a blade into the guy, you look his wife right in the
eye and repeat as needed. *I'm so sorry, truly sorry.*

It's helpful to think of it as a form of jazz, with varia-
tions on the basic riff.

Empathy is absolutely critical for a leader to have, according to my online executive coach Valerie Saint
Marco, whom I'm inclined to believe. "If they feel you
don't understand them, they'll lose respect."

She thinks I've recently taken over an accounting firm.

Valerie often talks about mirroring people's feelings
back to them. "You may not be familiar with the frustrations of a help-desk clerk or a first-year hire, for example,

but you can listen to their frustrations and mirror them back, showing you understand."

That bit really helped me; faking empathy is easy, but it's hard to know *when* to put the empathy in. Valerie's way of taking cues is excellent. I've noticed that some people want you to do an immediate leap to empathy, but with others, it's apparently more appropriate to go from anger to empathy along with them. You have to get that part right, or else they think your empathy is fake.

If people think you're faking empathy, that's worse than no empathy at all. Trust me on that.

I've found the mirroring thing also helps to make sure you don't empathize with the wrong things, because that's a sure sign that you're faking it.

So when I get to Valhalla, I ask Charles to tell me the story in his own words. It gives me a chance to figure out where to put the empathy regarding the nun situation. Charles is critical to the brothel operation, and I really need to keep him on board.

We're in his little office at the front of Valhalla, the small apartment complex positioned on the corner where a residential area gives way to a low-rent shopping and dining district. Dollar stores, that sort of thing. Charles is shaking with rage over the guard taking the nun.

So I do rage, too. I plan to kill the guard either way, but I'm angling to make it all about Charles. I set my face in a frown and show him my balled fists. Valerie says physical cues are 80% of your message. Who knew?

"That man needs to hurt," I say.

Charles nods, slowly.

The man is fixated on his nuns. He takes women to his home, dresses them in nun's outfits he's had specially made, and two weeks later they're hacked up and he needs another, because that last one wasn't quite right.

What the fuck are you supposed to do with that? I would defy even Valerie to feel empathy for this particular frustration.

But I need him running Valhalla. He was doing it under the old boss, Aldo Nikolla. Aldo himself would often say how fucking valuable Charles was. If I lose Charles's loyalty, I'll have to kill him, and there will be no one to run Valhalla. That would be a hell of a hit on the bottom line.

I know they don't see me as leader material. They see me more as an untrustworthy psycho who'll go bananas at the drop of a hat. That was part of Aldo Nikolla's PR, though I'll admit to doing my part to stoke it.

A *kumar* needs to instill fear. It's in the job description.

Aldo Nikolla made me heir apparent as a kind of insurance policy, knowing none of the ambitious *kryetar* would kill him and risk having me in charge.

Making a half-crazy, bloodthirsty killer your second-in-command...sure, it was a good plan for a man who didn't want the rank and file offing him.

But hello—when you make a bloodthirsty killer your heir, let's just say it's not the best longevity plan.

Needless to say, I was vague in explaining all of this to Valerie during our initial consultation.

Engaging an online coach—how desperate is that? But I was feeling desperate. I told her I wasn't a people person, that I didn't have the trust of my organization, but that I'd found myself in charge, asked whether she thought she could help.

She grasped the whole thing right away. "You're moving from a task-oriented role to a leadership role," she said. "It's common for people who excel in a support role to be thrust into leadership before they've developed the skills. And these first weeks are crucial. Your people are watching you."

I liked that she understood, and yeah, I know they are fucking watching me, a lot of them looking to defect, especially with the fucking Dragusha brothers out there.

"What do you think? I need those skills fast. Can I get to where I need to be? Get as good as my old boss fast enough?"

"Hell no," she said.

I was pretty fucking unhappy with this answer. Visions of tracking her down and breaking her neck danced through my head, but then she added, "I think you can be better than your old boss, Lazarus. I'm going to help you knock this fucker out of the park."

I felt such intense gratitude right then and there, which is saying a lot, because I don't tend to feel much. But for this I felt gratitude.

"Do you see what I did there, Lazarus?" she asked. "Give them a vision to believe in. Be their champion, and they'll be your champion. This is what I'll teach you to do, with actionable steps you can start taking right away."

Fucking Valerie. She's the shit.

Already her moves have been helping me. She's become my secret weapon. I'd be lying if I said I wasn't a little infatuated with her. She's hot in her picture, too. But I need to concentrate on the task at hand.

Valerie says that a leader who uses fear has a limited shelf life. Fear is effective at first, but the team will begin to chafe under the yoke of fear. I need to show them strength and understanding.

I sat there patiently as she delivered this particular message over our Skype connection, complete with a mixed metaphor that puts me on a shelf driving an oxen team. I've learned not to point out Valerie's mixed metaphors.

She's wrong about fear not being effective. Still, I can use this.

Cue the anger. I put my hand on Charles's shoulder, there in his messy office. "He will hurt," I say. We're in agreement there—the guard does need to hurt.

Charles seems to like this. So I start riffing. "We're going to find him," I say calmly. "And he is going to fucking beg to die. He is going to scream for me to end his life for what he did to you."

Charles nods. Valerie would be proud that I'm getting Charles's buy-in like this.

"And then I'm going to bring your nun back. Together we'll make Valhalla better and stronger."

"I need her unharmed," he says. "If she's harmed…"

"That's our goal," I say.

Heaven forbid she should be harmed before Charles can exercise his psychotic desires on her.

It's all so fucking exhausting.

It would be so much easier to squeeze the life out of Charles, what with his ridiculous nun fetish, which manages to be both pedestrian and absurd at the same time.

Valerie's website says that part of her job is being an executive confidante. She tells me she's there as my sounding board for confidences large and small, but Charles with his nun-killing fetish probably isn't the type of thing she has in mind.

I simply described Charles as a manager whose personality I'm not crazy about. Sometimes I think Valerie would get it, how really ridiculous and unimaginative the nun thing is, but she would fixate on the moral aspect of it to the exclusion of everything else. That would be so Valerie.

Anyway, the team is watching me for signs of how I'll champion them, so I'm making this thing about supporting Charles and the Valhalla team. Right there I can fucking see it working. Charles looks at me like I'm a warrior on his side instead of a vicious thug who shouldn't be running the massive criminal empire that is the Black Lion clan.

Lazarus 2.0 is a warrior for his people, Valerie once said. I like that. The 2.0 is cheesy, yeah, but when Valerie says it, it's not cheesy. When I complain about my antisocial image within the organization, she encourages me to invent a story for myself. *Maybe you were antisocial because that's what the role needed. Now you're not. You're a man who rises to the occasion.*

Valerie's excitement is infectious at times.

I sometimes wonder what will happen if the nun turns up dead. It was special for Charles that this woman actually was a nun, even though she wasn't an American nun. Can I find another nun? Will Charles accept another nun in her place? Is a hot nun like a puppy to a serial killer like Charles, where you can't just substitute them? Or is a hot nun more like a cookie, where one is as good as another? What's the more "champion of Charles" move?

More stuff that I can't ask Valerie.

First things first. Find the nun.

I want the nun back, and not just for Charles's sake. The nun's combination of blonde hair poking teasingly from her ridiculous head scarf and the way she never seemed to stop praying stoked the fervor and the bidding like I never saw. The rising price on her made her an excellent price anchor to the other girls, meaning she made them look cheap by comparison and raised the bidding all over. She also greatly raised the site's notoriety.

"You questioned the customer yourself?" I ask Charles. "The German who was here when the guard took her?"

Charles nods.

Charles would've been emotional, though, focused on his nun. He might not have been able to detect a lie. I may not have a very high emotional IQ—this per Valerie—but

I can cut through a lie like nobody else. I see clues nobody else sees.

Emotion makes people stupid. That's why I'm smart.

I need my hands on that German. "I'd like his contact information," I say. "Just in case."

Charles goes to his laptop and pulls up the spreadsheet. Nuns—*please*. Right?

That was his deal with Aldo Nikolla, though—he got to run his nun mania through Valhalla in lieu of payment. It makes him cheap, effective, and invested. Valerie would be proud.

He scribbles on a slip of paper and hands it over. "We don't think he has it in him," Charles says.

"People surprise you. But don't worry. This is our fucking town." I was about to say "my fucking town," but I changed it at the last second. "Our fucking town."

He's grateful.

Valerie. I'm getting addicted to her. So often I wish I could bring her into the mix, but I have to remind myself she's an executive coach, not a consigliore. Bringing Valerie in would be like wearing my shoe as a hat. Or would it?

In addition to finding the nun, I have to end the Dragusha brothers, do what Aldo Nikolla didn't have the balls to let me do all those nineteen years ago.

Everybody knows Aleksio and Viktor Dragusha are in play now. People are holding their breath, thinking the brothers will unite and take everything, just like in the prophecy.

Killing all of them would be ideal, but I only need one. It clearly has to be Kiro. I've tried sending people after Aleksio and Viktor, but it doesn't work out. My top guys won't touch that job—no fucking way. Aleksio and Viktor are too dangerous, too well-defended.

Killing Kiro will be easy once we find him.

Best of all, killing Kiro will solidify my leadership like nothing else. It's what my people need to see, like King Arthur pulling the sword from the stone.

Charles, in his anger, has people searching for the guard, but again, stupid. Where do frightened people go? They go where they feel safe. Where do people feel safe? Home. Where is home for a nun? A church.

I need Charles to get the idea. *Make your people feel smart,* Valerie always says. *You want them feeling good when they look in the mirror.*

I sit down with him and ask about his nun. He has a good deal of intel on her. He thinks she's smarter than she acts. She's from a convent out near the Russian-Ukrainian border called Svyataya Reka, which translates to Holy River, according to the internet. I ask him questions until he hits on the idea that she might seek out a church if she escapes from the guard. We do a little research together and locate a Russian Orthodox church on Leavitt Street. Very central, the largest in Chicago. And the names are similar.

"What do you think, Charles?"

"Tanechka will go there if she can," he informs me, quite pleased with himself. "They have nuns there, too. This is the one she'll pick."

I beam at him, mirroring his pleasure. "Awesome," I say. "Right. Then she'll lead us to him. Just in case, do you think we should post people at all of the Russian Orthodox churches in Chicago?"

"Better to be safe," he says.

"Good. Consider it done."

Well, it is done—I already have men at them, but he doesn't need to know.

The nun will escape—hopefully. Charles will get his victim to fuck with, like a Boy Scout with a spider; I'll make a bloody example of the guard; and it'll be a fucking coup.

I think.

Valerie sometimes sees angles that I don't. I really wish I could get Valerie's honest take.

But even if I kidnapped her, made her serve me that way, it probably wouldn't turn out. Or would it?

Ironically, Valerie would be the perfect person to ask about that, too.

CHAPTER TWELVE

Viktor

Tanechka is again locked in our bedroom. *Her* bedroom now. I let her have that. She can have anything she wants. *Almost anything.*

She can have anything the old Tanechka would want.

I head to the kitchen.

I learned what it was to suffer after I thought I'd killed her. This is hard in a different way.

But still so painful.

I twist the cap off a bottle of vodka, throw it across the room, and drink. The bottle won't be needing the cap anymore.

I collapse on the couch, head bowed, bottle dangling from my fingertips.

I trail over the afternoon in my mind, remembering her face as she bit into the honey cake. For a moment, she seemed like her.

When the bottle is half-gone, I go up the stairs to check on her. It's quiet. I put my ear to the door.

"Go away," she calls out. "Leave me."

"I'll never leave you, *lisichka*."

Silence.

I slide down to the floor outside the room, sitting with my back to the door. She hates me. She should, of course. Especially if she gets her memory back.

For now, all I can do is to show her that she isn't alone. "I love you beyond anything," I say.

Nothing.

I take another swig, letting the liquid coat my throat against the darkness of memory. She's all alone in there. Upset. Every sound she makes is a blade to my belly.

"You'll never be alone," I say. "I'll always be here, a dog at your feet."

A sniffling sound. Is she crying?

I press the heels of my palms into my eyes. Guilt and self-loathing mix together into a familiar cocktail, churning in my chest.

If only she'd been taken in by farmers or a government clerk. Anybody but nuns.

And the woman with the ring *was* an assassin, after all. Her death saved lives. Tanechka's god should care about that.

I can bear it no longer. I stand. I pound. "Let me in."

"Leave me."

I throw the bottle at the door the end of the hall. It shatters. I feel half-blind.

"Tanechka!"

No answer.

I heave my shoulder against the door and break it open. She's sitting on the bed, scarf askew, bright hair wild, eyes red.

CHAPTER THIRTEEN

Tanechka

He's a beautiful beast, hands gripping my shoulders. "The incident of the ring is one small part of your life," he says.

"The *incident*? I killed a woman!"

"She was an assassin, *lisichka*."

I shake my head. "It's not for me to pass judgment. That's only for God, Viktor."

He hauls me up and pushes me against the wall. "You will stop with this talk of God!"

"I'll talk about whatever I want."

He heaves out a breath, nostrils flaring. I should be frightened, but so much about him is deeply familiar. Pleasant, even.

I shouldn't feel bad for him. I shouldn't feel breathless when he holds me against the wall.

"Your god doesn't know you—not like I do." His heat grows. He thrums with intensity, scruffy cheeks glinting in the light of the bedside lamp. He hasn't shaved.

He forgets to shave when he's upset. The thought bubbles up in from nowhere and makes me want to take his head to my breast and comfort him. I tell myself it means nothing. I don't know him.

"Your god will never know you as I do, Tanechka, and he'll *never, ever* love you as I do."

"You're wrong." I push him away and stand on my own, panting. "God loves me unconditionally. Do you?"

"Yes!"

"Unless I'm a nun."

"I love you for who you are." Still his gaze bores into me.

The thought comes to me that he'll do something crazy now. He's like a song—I know every note before it is sung. I brace myself.

Snarling, he grabs either side of his white shirt and rips it open, revealing his hard, muscular chest, spattered with dark hair. I see the inky swirls and letters over his heart, the tattoo to match mine: "Tanechka + Viktor." "You have the same."

I clutch the fabric at my breast.

"No." He pushes my arms away, grabs my collar, and rips my robe down the middle. The tattoo peeks out from under the cotton shift that covers my thin slip. With a look of horror he yanks the shift down to reveal the entirety of the tattoo. "They tried to bleach it. Who did this? Not the nuns. The men at Valhalla? Who touched you?"

I try to push him away. I fail.

"Who? I'll kill him."

"Then I won't tell you."

"I'll kill them all." He traces it with a trembling finger. "Did it hurt?"

"No."

"This is how they knew your name."

"Leave me."

"They couldn't get rid of it completely."

"They would've, and I was glad. I wanted it gone." The sisters liked to pretend it wasn't there, as did I. Another life, another person.

I stiffen as Viktor presses his lips to the tattoo, leaves them pressed there over my pounding heart.

I try to push him away. It's like pushing a mountain.

"God doesn't know you like I do, or he'd love everything about you, and everything you ever did." He presses his lips to my shoulder, to the to the upper curve of my breast as he says this, as if he'd speak directly to my heart. "If God knew you like I did, he'd be crazy in love with you."

"Don't talk like that."

With a growl he draws away, dark eyes even wilder. He grabs my shift and tears it down the middle.

Heat flashes through me.

He pushes the remaining bits of robe and shift over my right shoulder, so that it's like a coat half-on, revealing my slip.

I push at him futilely, garments hanging from my other shoulder. I fear he'll rip my slip off, too, and take my nipple in my mouth.

The image spears me with warmth. How could I want such things?

Instead, he sets his finger on a scar at the far side of my collarbone. Was this his goal? To reveal this scar? And not my nipple?

"Did you ever notice how many of your scars are crosshatched, Tanechka?"

I pant, keenly aware of his soft, warm fingers.

"Have you noticed?"

"I don't think about them. The scars are ugly reminders of another life."

"They're beautiful." He grabs my arm and jerks it up so that I'm face to face with another ugly scar, this one on the underside of my forearm. "Crosshatched. Look at it, Tanechka!"

I turn my eyes to it. Anything to end this.

"A defensive wound. The crosshatching shows that the scar was made when you were very young." His gaze is fierce with soul. "It's what happens when the skin stretches over it as the body grows. This one you got when you were ten, defending a child in your housing block from a sadistic teenaged predator."

His fingers move along the raised ridges of the scar as if it speaks a language only he can divine.

Magic grows in the space between us.

"You threw yourself into danger so that the weaker child could get away. You were like this, Tanechka. Even in the brothel. You wanted to take the pain for those women. This is who you are—this! This scar is who you are, true and fierce."

I clutch the brown serge to my shoulder. I'd always imagined it was something dark and despicable, that scar. "Nothing erases being a killer."

"You need to know who you were before you say that." He pulls at the fabric. This is a battle I won't win—he's stronger and has the advantage of knowing I won't truly hurt him.

There's no sense allowing him to rip my robe more, so I push him away and cast off the rest of my outer garments. "Happy?"

I tremble before him in nothing but a thin, nearly see-through slip and panties. My tunic is a heap at my feet. It'll take forever to sew it back up. I focus on that. I'll get a needle and thread and sew it back up.

"Do what you will," I continue. "I was prepared for as much at the brothel."

He looks devastated. "You think I'd hurt you like that?" He presses gentle fingers over the fabric of the slip, pressing it to the place where my ribcage turns to soft belly. I stiffen as I realize what he's going for—two long white scars, a double scar like train tracks curling around my side. They become visible when he presses the fabric around them.

"You got this rescuing a puppy from barbed wire. Your father beat you for your trouble, as you knew he would, but you did it anyway. There was no vulnerable being you wouldn't fight for. Your father was drunk and weak, but you were strong. You were the head of your little family, even caring for your father, much as you disdained him."

My pulse races. His nearness affects me deeply. The way he knows everything about me is seductive. All of these things I dreaded. They're not all bad.

"And here…" He presses two fingers to a spot on my ribs that sometimes aches. "At the age of fourteen you confronted the police who were demanding protection money from a friend, a poor girl who spent all of her money to bury her baby son, who'd just died. The police beat you with clubs and shattered this rib. They said you attacked them. You probably did. You hated the police, and you hated Putin and his people. This landed you in a home for bad girls." He grazes his fingertips over the spot. "It hurts in the rain and snow. A heating pad helps. I have one. I'll bring it to you and show you how you used it."

He's right. It does hurt when it rains.

"I know your body as my own, *lisichka,*" he whispers. "It once *was* my own, just like my body was yours. Even now, everything I am is for you."

The dark pull of him is getting stronger.

He moves his hand to my side, to the angriest, worst scar of all. The bullet—even the nuns knew I'd been shot there. There's an exit wound behind.

Viktor drops to his knees, lips an inch from this ugly, ugly wound. He presses the thin fabric of the slip to it so that it shows through, and he traces around it with his finger. His finger thick and blunt. With his other hand he touches my hip.

I grip against the sweetness of it.

"The doctor said you should keep it moist. With coconut oil. I'll bring you some."

I nod, heart in my throat.

He traces around it again. I suck in a breath, focusing my mind on the repairs I must do on the garments he ripped. I imagine the types of stitches I'll use—anything to take my mind off his tender touch.

But he's hard to ignore, this clothed and powerful man on his knees before me. I'm aware of his roughness against my bare skin.

He makes my belly quiver. My breathing speeds. I don't want him to stop. I dream of being a nun and taking a vow of chastity, yet here I stand, loving a killer's touch.

He touches the center of the scar, and I stiffen. Because now he has to kiss it there. That's the game. Touch and kiss. "Please, no," I gasp.

Eyes turned up at me, he brings his lips to it. Softly, gently. His kiss is silky and electric.

"This is where you saved my life. You took this bullet for me, Tanechka."

He clutches my hips, kisses me again, so soft I can barely detect it.

"I hated you for doing it. It was during our war with the Petrov gang. They were going to kill me, and you hurled yourself at Roman Petrov like a wild animal. And then the gun went off, and when I saw you crumple over, my whole life dissolved before my eyes. We were so frightened for you, Yuri and I. We took you to the hospital in their territory—it couldn't be helped. We guarded you until we could move you. We didn't think any of us would survive."

He pushes his face to my belly. He clutches the backs of my thighs through my slip.

My hands go to his hair.

"We were so frightened for you. Pityr kidnapped a doctor to give a second opinion, so crazy. You were sick for so long afterwards, but we got you back. You came back to us."

My belly seems to move of its own accord, too much alive. He closes his eyes and kisses me again through the fabric. My sex feels floaty.

He squeezes the backs of my thighs, fingers biting into the thin cotton. A glowy good feeling rolls up between my legs as he turns his face up, kneading my thighs ever so slightly.

I tighten my fists in his hair. I should push him off.

I'll push him off soon.

He turns his face back to my belly and tips his head down so that his mouth is level with my sex, but he doesn't touch me. "You always loved it when I talked here, breathed here. You loved to feel the close space between us. You always loved the space where nothing and everything happens—the space between, you called it. You were fascinated with this."

I close my eyes, enjoying of the heat from his mouth. Aware also of the answering heat from between my legs.

"You loved when I almost kissed you there," he says. "When I almost touched you. Almost licked you. You loved that. I had only to touch you here to end you."

He touches the fabric between my legs. The fabric doesn't connect to any part of my body, just to the space between my legs.

I'm faint with feeling. He touched there and now he has to kiss it.

I push him away. "I don't play your games anymore."

He rolls back on his heels, gazing up, beautiful eyes warm and sparkling. "You would feel everything. So sensitive. The game would make you feel everything."

"Leave me."

He rises to his feet. "One touch of my finger and you'd come apart screaming…"

I gather my garments. "Look what you did. It'll take hours to sew."

"You're not sewing it. This costume isn't for you." He rips my robe and the rest of it from my hands, yanks my scarf from my head, and storms off.

I chase after him. "Viktor, please!"

Down the stairs he goes.

"Viktor!"

He stalks through the living room to the fireplace, where embers still glow. He tosses it in. I dart after it, but he grabs me my arm, fingers digging into my flesh. With his free hand he takes a poker and shoves at the burning fabric, shoving it around over the embers. I watch in despair as my garments go up in flames.

Finally, he lets me go.

I fall to my knees in front of the fireplace.

"There's a closet full of clothes for you up there. Beautiful clothes you once loved. You'll wear those. You'll wear the clothes of Tanechka from now on."

CHAPTER FOURTEEN

Viktor

S he tromps down the stairs the next morning in a T-shirt and jeans, bright hair flowing over her shoulders. The breath goes out of me. "*Lisichka.*"

She continues toward me, big black boots clomping. "Don't get used to it. I'll be back in the serge robe soon. You can't stop me from it."

I smile. She chose those clothes for a breakout.

I understand her the way a sailor understands the ocean.

She'll pull a knit cap over her head and tuck in her hair as soon as I'm gone. Then she'll don a black jacket filled with whatever rope she can find. Other supplies. The old Tanechka would carve up the treads of the boots for better gripping. I would give anything to go with her, to be allies again.

Instead, I'll have my men stop her.

On my way out, I stop Pityr, one of the guys I have guarding the street. He's on edge. I clap him on the back. "*Blatnye*," I say.

He's not feeling so *blatnye*, so badass. He addresses me in Russian. "Bloody Lazarus's *patsani* just passed by. Three cars." He lifts his phone. "Everybody's been texting about it."

I clench my jaw. "What was your impression?"

"They don't know about your place," he says, grasping the direction of my thoughts. "They've been crawling up and down every street, daring us to engage. Suggesting that this is their town. A show of force. They'll do something here soon. A new leader needs to exert power."

I nod. "Agreed."

"I don't know why they haven't already," he says. "Maybe he wants to keep his cops happy." He uses the word *mussor*—"garbage"—but he really means cops.

"Bloody Lazarus doesn't care about keeping anybody happy. It's why he'll be easy to take down."

"They're saying Lazarus is a decent leader. Everybody's surprised." He fills me in on the rumors that the rabid killer thing was only an act; now that he's taken over the family, Lazarus is clever and thoughtful.

The Russian guys say Lazarus was giving bonuses to all young American Russian warriors who would defect to him. He tells me the American Russians are getting jumpy about it. Unhappy that gang war might break out.

"We came into this neighborhood to get more solid with them. *Blyad*—what if we're alienating them?" I say.

Pityr shakes his head. "Dunno, *brat*."

"If the wrong person defects, we're fucked."

He nods.

Aleksio won't like this. I point to the roof, the path Tanechka would take. "She's going to try going high. You remember how well she could do that?"

"So fast and light," he says. "The nun skirt'll hinder."

"She changed out of it."

He raises his eyebrows. He thinks it's a good sign.

"Don't underestimate her. And call me if anything happens. Even insignificant."

I call Yuri and Tito and tell them what's happening. They need to be ready—especially with Lazarus's people crawling around.

Aleksio is waiting at the Tiptop Diner some ten blocks away. I slide into the booth across from him and tell him what Pityr said about Bloody Lazarus. All the bratki rallying around him.

"I don't get it. They're just cool with the whole psycho thing?"

"They're saying the psycho thing was an act," I tell him. "They're saying Bloody Lazarus became what he needed to when he was enforcer and now that he's leader, he's no longer a psycho."

"So he's gone from John Wayne Gacy to Jeff Bezos?"

I shrug. I don't know these names. I order orange juice.

"Fuck. If the American Russian gang starts losing guys to *Bloody Lazarus*? That's bad," he says once the waitress leaves.

"Back home, the only way out of a gang is feet first."

Aleksio snorts. "We need to start bonding with the Russians here more. We need to start spreading more money around. And I missed that fucking sit-down with Dmitri yesterday."

"*Blyad!* You can't miss meetings with their leader." Dmitri is the leader of them.

"It was an emergency. I had to."

"We need their loyalty if we're going to fight Lazarus."

"We'll do better," he says.

I nod and look out the diner window. We're both anxious to hear about Kiro, but we don't want to jinx it by discussing it. I ask about Konstantin. "I want him to meet Tanechka," I say. "I never got to bring a girl home to my family. Konstantin, he's the grumpy grandfather I never had. The grumpy Albanian grandpa with his shit Turkish coffee."

"Shows you don't know dick about coffee." He checks his phone. The P.I. is late. A bad sign.

If Bloody Lazarus got to our P.I., it means the P.I. is dead and they probably have the information he was after. And a way to Kiro.

I get my juice. I sip. "We could find Kiro today. That's the other side of it."

He looks at me with interest.

"What?"

"Look at you, Susie Sunshine."

It is unlike me, I suppose, to look at the bright side, as they say. But Tanechka's back. Anything's possible.

"But you're right. We'll find Kiro, and if he's in a supermax, then we'll be the first motherfuckers to break a man out of a supermax." He eyes me. "How *is* Tanechka?"

"Adjusting." I picture her walking down the stairs in her regular clothes, hair fanned out over her shoulders. Eyes shining with challenge. It was almost her. "She knows about some of the...things she did."

"Things. Meaning *hits*?" I nod. "Shit. How's she taking it?"

"Not so good. I didn't mean for her to know yet. At least she's wearing normal clothes now. T-shirt and jeans. So nice to see her in that."

He straightens. "She changed out of her nun's outfit? How'd you get her to do that?"

"It wasn't exactly voluntary."

"Viktor, what the fuck are you doing? What happened to surrounding her with familiar things and letting her go at her own pace?"

I shrug.

He unwraps a straw and shoves it into his soda. "I didn't respect what Mira wanted, and I almost lost her."

"Your Mira was not in the home you bought for her kissing the feet of another man."

He furrows his brow. "Another man?"

"Jesus."

He gives me a look. "Dude."

"What? You say I should respect her, this *is* about respect—respect of who Tanechka truly is. She wouldn't want this. Tanechka would expect me to fight for her. I'd die to have her back in the world."

"What if that is Tanechka?"

"It's not. You didn't know her. She deserves at least to remember who she was, so she can make a choice."

"Are you giving her a choice? I mean, I get it, Viktor, a nun is a hard limit..."

But suddenly Sykes, our P.I., is there, hat shoved down over his head.

Aleksio slides in next to me so the man can have the other side of the booth to himself.

"Not loving this public place," Sykes grumbles.

Aleksio slides him cash, and he spins a thumb drive across the table to us. He has a wide face, a small nose, and skin the color of American spray tan. "That's the filings. A lot of bullshit in there, just so you can see what I did. I got Kiro's report. That's the good news."

That gets our attention.

"He got arrested, all right," Sykes says. "It's pretty much the story you heard—he attacked the officers who freed him—attacked without provocation. Guy really fucking went to town. Guy doesn't like to be restrained."

He sits back and slides his hands to either side of him. This P.I. Sykes, he's a man who takes up two seats when he can.

"Bad news: He went before district court, and they had a sanity hearing. Apparently he was committed, but I can't get anything definitive, and certainly not where he was sent. A certificate of commitment was created at some point, but it's been deleted on corresponding spreadsheets. I have one more idea, but it'll take another round of FOIA filings. I went ahead and did that."

"Hold on—committed?" Aleksio says. "As in, an insane asylum?"

"Possibly. They had a hearing with two lawyers—one for the state, one for him—and a psychiatrist. It's procedure in a commitment case. I've got the lawyer's name, but he retired soon after. I'm tracking him down. I'm guessing you want me to put the hurt on him."

"Do whatever it takes to make him talk," Aleksio says.

"Something strange, though—the psychiatrist's name was blacked out. And the hard copies were filled out with a different font than other papers in the batch."

"What does that mean?" Aleksio asks.

"Could be a lot of reasons for that. Some innocent, some fishy. Thing is, he went to town on all those cops. My guess is that he's in the system somewhere on an MI and D—mentally ill and dangerous—but where? That's why I did the other filing."

"Meaning he may be in a prison for the criminally insane," Aleksio says.

I hiss out a breath. "Rotting in a lunatic asylum?"

"It could be that, we just don't know," Sykes says.

"It's not as bad here as in Russia," Aleksio says.

I growl. It's all bad.

"He could've been in for a term and then released to a halfway house," Sykes continues. "I'm going as fast as I can here. You said not to draw attention. There are difficult personalities involved down at the records desk. Buying a fucking vanilla frappé for the desk guy. Like a fucking little megalomaniac behind his fucking desk."

I feel rage flare hot in my head. I speak through clenched teeth. "What is this man's name, please."

The P.I. glances nervously at Aleksio, who holds up a hand, as if that will calm me. "We have a legal right to this information," Aleksio says. "He won't hand it over?"

"Laws are only as fair as those enforcing them."

Now Aleksio growls.

"Take a chill pill, guys," Sykes says. "I'm on it."

I turn to Sykes. "Did you see signs of anyone else poking around?"

"I'd tell you if I did," he says. "My writer-doing-research cover looks legit. I have a book on Amazon."

I take a deep breath, trying to be the man Kiro needs me to be. "We need to get our facts before acting." I say this to myself more than anybody else. I eye my brother. "If we act rashly now, we could be sorry forever." I don't really feel it, but I say it.

Aleksio meets my gaze. A lump forms in my throat because I know he's thinking about me and Tanechka, too.

"Fuck me," Aleksio whispers. "Don't look around."

I stiffen.

"We're being watched," he says.

This is bad.

"Fucking hell." I find my piece and set it in my lap, flicking off the safety.

Sykes sucks in a breath. "What the fuck? Will they move on us?"

"Depends," Aleksio says. "And they've seen us together now. Dammit. How long does it take them to put a name and address to your face?"

"Not fucking long," Sykes growls. He begins to get up.

I clamp a hand over his wrist. He's shaking. "Where're you going?"

"The fuck out of here."

"No. Our orders now. We think how to get out of here, then figure where to put you."

"Because you can't go back to your place," Aleksio says.

"What? I have a dog," Sykes says.

"Gimme your address, we'll get your dog. Hurry," Aleksio says.

"I can't *not* go home."

"We got places," Aleksio says. "It's cool."

"It's not *cool*," Sykes says.

"You prefer interrogation? At the hands of Bloody Lazarus, maybe? No. You'll keep investigating from a safe place we put you in. We'll send a tail to keep you safe. You will stay on the job," Aleksio says.

Sykes is scared and pissed. He gives his address, voice shaking. Aleksio pulls out his phone and texts Tito to grab the dog and the things Sykes wants from his house.

"Are you guys not worried your enemies are out there to gun us down?"

"We don't know what their plan is." Aleksio's phone vibrates. He checks the screen. "Tito and Nikki'll get the dog." He looks up at me. "*Together*. That's interesting."

"My dog's gonna freak out if strangers come and take him."

"Tito knows how to handle dogs. He'll bring meat." He looks up at me. "We have to split up. I'll get Sykes out. You come around back and cover us if need be. We'll pretend not to notice them unless they make a move."

"Running from a fight like *kozel*," I say. "Like goats. I don't like it. I could come up behind. *Pop*."

"Viktor, no. We don't even see them, got it?" Aleksio says. "We have to hurry before they get backup."

"They're in our face. They followed one of us, they drive our streets. We need to hit back."

"Not the time," he says. "Maybe we'll find something to do after this." He gives me a significant look that I understand immediately. He means we'll do something on their money-laundering business. That works. I feel like getting bloody.

"You're going with me in my car," Aleksio tells Sykes. "Viktor'll ride your motorcycle. Give him your keys."

"And I do what you say or else?" Sykes complains. "Is that the situation here?"

"Yeah, that's the situation," he says, low and threatening.

The P.I. hands over his keys and his hat.

It'll feel good to ride on a motorcycle. I'll ride fast, and maybe the wind will blow some of Tanechka from my mind.

I fix Sykes with my own hard look. "Move with calm confidence out to the car. That's the feeling that you want to show."

Aleksio smiles at me. He loves when I talk like that. So much of *blatnoy* warfare is image.

"I'll see you at that McDonald's," Aleksio says.

I nod. There's a McDonald's near the money-laundering warehouse.

I head to the bathroom and slip out the window, piece drawn.

Nobody's in back. Maybe it really is just two guys. Spotted one of us.

I ride Sykes's bike to a snaggle-toothed industrial zone southwest of downtown and pull into the McDonald's. Aleksio shows up with Yuri after a while. We ditch the car and bike in the shadows and go on foot to the textile warehouse with the broken lookout chimney.

This textile warehouse is next to Lazarus's main money-laundering node—where cash is collected. They launder it with an import scheme. An old technique.

This chimney gives us a perfect view of everything that goes on there. If we hit his operation when coffers are full, he'll be reeling for weeks.

The textile warehouse security guard we threatened is not happy to see us. We proceed on in to the back room and call up to Santino, the man Aleksio posted. Italian. New muscle from Milwaukee.

Santino *is* happy to see us. He opens his laptop and shows us the footage he's taken from his perch, many photos in different light. He created a PowerPoint program that shows the guard roster and details. Aleksio and his *patsanis*, they love their charts and bullet points.

- Guards switch shifts at ten
- #2 smokes five times per shift
- Five men in all.

"We should make our move soon," Aleksio says. "Before they change locations."

I direct Santino to the backup to the photos. Once they're up on the screen, I point to a sliver of light on the roof. "Is this an opening?"

"I thought it was a reflection," Santino says. "But wait..."

We compare it to other shots and arrange the night shots in a row on the screen. "Fuck me," he says. "It's an opening on the roof."

It'll be dark soon. I suggest we grab a cable camera and try to lower it in there.

Aleksio swallows. "Climb right up on their roof? Motherfuck." He likes it.

I'm liking it, too. "But your ankle..."

Aleksio waves it off.

"I don't see you getting up there undetected," Santino says.

"We will, and you're going to cover us," Aleksio says. "If we can get a visual inside there it would be a cakewalk to hit."

I nod. We could go in soon. Rob the shit out of Lazarus.

It'll feel good to hurt him.

Aleksio smiles at me.

Two hours later we're stealing through the dark with cameras and rock-climbing gear. He's still limping, but that's Aleksio. Always ready. "Konstantin would not like this," he says.

"I know," I say. But Konstantin isn't in charge.

We cut a rusted fence. It's a fuck of a dangerous thing, going in this way. But both of our imaginations were seized by that sliver of light and the promise of getting eyes in there.

It could take a week or even a month to cripple Valhalla, but hitting this place will take Lazarus's attention away from Kiro. It may even make him lose his cool. If he loses his cool, he loses his people.

We crouch in the dark. "We really need to get out more often."

I smirk.

When Santino gives the flash signal, we rush up and begin to scale the side of the building. Tilt-concrete construction. The surface is rough with few handholds.

This part is dangerous; not so much for falling, but if caught, we are so easy to shoot. Santino is in the chimney next door, covering us with a long-range rifle. It'll help. A little.

We scramble onto the roof, out of breath. Quietly we pull up the gear. If we make noise, we'll have to rappel down. Again, easy to shoot.

We lie side by side on the soft, still-warm rubberized surface of the roof. The stars are bright, the air thin.

"When we hit this place, we should bring some of the American Russians," Aleksio says. "We let them keep all the money."

"Good idea," I say.

We crawl on our bellies toward the mechanical plant. The sliver hole will be in the seal around the HVAC equipment.

Creeeeeeak.

I freeze and shut my eyes. It was loud—much too loud. It's not just about the dangerous people inside; the roof may be unstable.

I catch Aleksio's eye. He shakes his head and pulls out his phone to call Santino. Nobody coming. We're okay. For now.

Santino thinks we should come back. The roof sags ahead; it'll mean more creaking.

"Fuck that," Aleksio whispers. He points out a slight ridge. That would be the support. "We'll be safe if we stay right on that."

A lot of tundra to cross. Fifty feet, perhaps.

We crawl slowly, head to toe now, Aleksio in front. The massive mechanicals that supply heat to the space below are housed up ahead in silver casing.

He reaches the plant first and opens his pack.

The camera is on the end of a small cable. He unspools it, fits it into the hold, and lowers it.

I come up next to him and watch the view on my phone. It's a long process.

"Still, there's one thing I've been wondering," he says, unspooling it one centimeter at a time, lowering it down into the space. He twists to change the view.

I peer through the lens via my iPhone. "Keep going."

He unspools it more. "Your endgame." He continues to work calmly. "What's your endgame with Tanechka?"

"If nothing else works, she'll eventually want to fuck. She could never resist me. Once we fuck, she'll for sure remember. Her body will tell her who I am, who she is."

"That's your endgame? To make her want you? And you fuck her memory back?"

"She's a *nun* with Jesus as her imaginary friend. I can't let her stay like that."

"So let's play this out. You're fucking her, and that's when she remembers she's a stone-cold killer instead of a nun."

"Exactly."

"Fucking a woman who could, at any moment, remember she's a trained assassin who wants to kill you. That's your endgame."

"It's under control," I growl.

"No, Viktor, it's the opposite of under control. It's an unconscious agenda that's controlling *you*."

"You Americans," I spit. "You American and your psychological cotton candy," I say, unable to find a better word. "Just cotton candy."

"No, I'm onto something. You're telling her everything about your old life except for one important detail."

I give him a look, there in the dark.

"What's the one thing you aren't telling her?"

"Fuck off," I say.

"The one thing you're not telling her is that you *threw her over that cliff.*" He whisper-shouts that last phrase. "Why not tell the nun about that? You're telling her everything else. You told her she's a killer. How much worse would it be to tell her you tried to kill her?"

"It's too much," I say.

"Bullshit," Aleksio says. "You don't want the nun to know because the nun might forgive you. And that's the last thing you want, isn't it?"

My head swims.

"You don't want forgiveness. You want the assassin to kill you." He unspools the line. "This is a fucking death wish is what this is."

"If I wanted to die I'd be dead already," I growl, pulling up the images on the app. All dark.

"But you don't want to just die. You want Tanechka to kill you."

I snort, concentrating on the feed from the camera now inside the warehouse.

Is he right?

"Let me ask you a question—how would it feel if she plunged a blade into your gut?"

I freeze, stunned by the question.

"Come on, be honest."

I imagine her coming after me with a blade. I imagine her sinking it under my ribs and...it feels right. Good. *Warm*, somehow.

The world went cold the day I killed her. Her blade in my belly would make it warm again. Right again.

I don't know what to think—not about anything. So I focus on the picture. Shapes. The full room comes into view. "I'm seeing something."

He doesn't reply.

I look up to find him glaring.

"It's bullshit," he says. "Maybe I'll tell her."

"Don't." I make an adjustment in the cable.

He clamps a hand over my arm. "You want Tanechka to punish you. But you've punished yourself enough."

"I should've believed in her," I say.

"Tell Tanechka that. Tell her while she's still a nun. Promise me you won't fuck her until you tell her what you did."

The silence between us stretches long and wide.

I think again about her blade, sliding between my ribs, piercing my heart.

I wonder to myself what it would feel like.

Maybe it would feel like freedom.

CHAPTER FIFTEEN

Tanechka

The strangest sense of familiarity passes over me as I sneak along the rooftop, night wind in my hair.

The men below are good; they know to look up. They had one man stationed on the roof, but he went down for a piss break. He should've pissed on the roof.

I race along and jump the short gap to the next roof, a deeply familiar move. I know not to look down. I know how to land, setting my weight forward.

My plan is to run to the Orthodox church I found in the phone book in the kitchen. These guys are so careful about keeping me away from phones and the internet, they forgot about paper. A Russian Orthodox church not twenty blocks away, judging from the map at the back. Very large. The name is Sacred River—very similar to our Svyataya Reka, Holy River. There are nuns there. My people. I'll tell them about the virgin brothel, and we'll

175

identify police we can trust. We'll get them involved in rescuing the girls. And I'll contact the sisters overseas.

And get away from Viktor.

He's too much. He gets near me and my defenses crumble. I need to put a world between us.

I race across, leaping again, landing lightly. I feel strong and small and good.

I pause and take in a breath, then I slip down the side of a peaked roof and grab onto a tree, clinging to the branch. I fumble for a foothold and quickly descend. I rustle the branches, but never mind; I'll vanish before anybody can get to the window.

I hit the ground and take off, racing through the night streets toward the church.

I feel eyes all around. A person watching you is a feeling, always a feeling.

I turn a corner and walk; it's time to blend. I hate that I know this. A nun wouldn't know this. I tell myself things will be all right. When I used to worry about my violent past, Mother Olga would say that God loves all his children, especially the difficult ones.

I'm one of the difficult ones.

Footsteps. I'm being followed. I slip around the corner of a brownstone and hide.

Somebody coming. Three men.

I set off running in the other direction, though unfamiliar streets. I can feel danger growing. It's a feeling on my skin. In the air.

I cut through a gloomy alley. I don't know this place. I don't like it. I move through the shadows and peek out. Empty sidewalk.

I turn out, begin to walk.

Hands grab me from behind and pull me back. I'm shoved face-first into the rough, cool side of a building.

My cheek grazes the brick. My heart pounds.

A whisper in my ear, soft as a feather. "You used to like it like this."

Viktor.

He presses into me. I feel melty inside.

"I'd shove you up to a wall just like this. I'd take you from behind. Use you hard like a stranger."

He presses harder. Something in me trembles.

Desire.

"I'd make you turn your head and open your eyes so I could see what I did to you."

"I'm different now," I whisper.

"Are you?" Roughly he turns me to face him.

My pulse races. *Am I?* "Leave me. Let me be with my people."

"To your pathetic church? Your god up in the sky? Like Mickey Mouse? I'm your people." He's furious and beautiful.

I glare at him harshly. It only seems to make him happy.

"Come on." He drags me back. No use fighting now; the street is filled with his fighters.

Ten minutes later we're back in the apartment.

Once again I'm upstairs in the large bedroom. I'm on a thick bearskin rug in front of the roaring fire, in fact.

That sounds nice, I suppose. It would be nice if my ankle weren't shackled to a chain that goes to a fat metal heating pipe that runs up and down the wall. Just enough room to go and lie in front of the fire, or to use the small, windowless bathroom.

Viktor gives it a tug and steps back. The part that connects to my ankle is an iron cuff with a padlock. The fire crackles.

"How is this different from the brothel?" I ask. "Kept for a man's whim?"

"Utterly different." He lifts a corner of the rug and peers underneath, then he stands and swishes through the coin dish on the dresser. He's looking for things I can use to pick the lock—hard, bendable things. As if I can remember how to pick a lock. Then again, I know exactly what he's looking for, so perhaps I do know.

I certainly knew how to traverse rooftops.

He says, "You're lucky I grabbed you first. Because you know who else is out there looking for you? Bloody Lazarus. Remember? The man who owns Valhalla? His men are on the hunt for you. What do you think he'll do when he finds you? Your experience with him will be very different from your experience with me. He'll probably bring you back to that Charles guy."

Shivers roll over my skin. "I was grateful it was me dining with Charles and not one of the other girls."

Viktor unscrews the door stopper and tosses it out of the range of my chain. He yanks up a piece of molding, and I get the feeling it's just to get the nail out of my range. He thinks I could use a nail?

"Nothing will stop me from going back where I belong, Viktor. Not you, not Lazarus."

"You think Lazarus can't stop you? Even Tanechka at the height of her powers wasn't magical." His look is dark. It scares me a little. "We always knew he was bloodthirsty. We never knew he was smart."

I lie back. "Still. I will leave again."

"The old Tanechka wouldn't run through the streets to a predictable destination. So predictable. Running to a church." He practically spits out the word.

"Maybe Tanechka *should've* run to a church."

"Tanechka was perfect. She didn't need a church."

He kneels at my feet and tucks a sock around the inside of my leg iron, on the outside of my jeans. Cushioning the metal. Roughness and softness. Harshness and care.

A familiar thrill of excitement rushes over me. He looks up, catches it in my gaze. "I like this. You all chained up for me."

"You need to let me go," I say. "I need to confess what I've done."

He sniffs.

"I killed a person."

"Perhaps. Or is it all lies? It's too bad you can't remember. Tanechka would."

"Viktor, please. I can't be what you want."

"Then you'll die of old age in this room."

"You killed, too," I say. "Don't you want to find some peace?"

This seems to stop him. I see heat in his face. Rage. Or maybe shame. "It's too late for me."

"How do you live with it?"

He seems to consider this. "It hurts sometimes. But you go forward." He kneels in front of me. "We've always been fighters, Tanechka. We've always been dark and wrong. When you don't expect sunshine and happiness, nothing can hurt you." He tucks in another sock, cushioning my ankle all around. "Hell is only disappointing to those who were expecting heaven."

I look over at the icon of Jesus. Too far to reach.

"Don't even think of asking. You don't get to kiss him anymore."

"It doesn't matter. Take it away—you won't change my heart. I saw light shine from his eyes. You can't take that away from me. The sweetest, brightest light you can ever imagine."

"I grow weary of your fairy tales." He gets up and walks out.

"Viktor!" I call.

Nothing.

I inspect the chain. I yank on it. I test the strength of the pipe. Nothing. I run my hand across the thick, rich fur of the rug. So decadent. We didn't have such things at the convent. Yet the familiarity of it goes deep into my bones.

Fur in front of a fire—is this like the honey cake? The American rock and roll?

I shove the rug away and sit on the hardwood floor.

I turn to the bookshelf across the room where I set the small icon. I can't reach it, but I can gaze upon it.

He returns with a tray loaded with pears and cherries. My heart lifts. And then falls. I know this trick.

"You keep feeding me Tanechka food. It won't work."

He says nothing about the rug bunched up by the wall. He simply sets down the tray, stokes up the fire, and sits cross-legged beside me.

"You remembered how to escape along a roof." He takes the pear. Something silver flashes in his other hand. There's a tickle in my palm.

He watches me with glittering eyes. He flicks the catch, and the blade snaps out.

My mouth goes dry. I can feel the shiver of that snap, the weight of it. The sharp power of it.

"You remember it, don't you? It's just like yours."

I look away.

"You used to be able to do a lot of damage with one of these things." He cuts into the pear. I watch it drip, so juicy, this pear. He passes me a slice.

I shake my head.

"Eat it or I'll sit on top of you and shove it into your mouth."

I sigh and take it, not wanting to give him any more opportunities for contact. It's powerful enough to have him near me, to have this electricity dancing between us. I take the pear slice. It's delicious, like all of the food he feeds me.

He slices another, then looks up at me and smiles his wicked and gorgeous smile.

CHAPTER SIXTEEN

Viktor

She recognized it instantly.

Her favorite blade, the R-37 with the silver barrel handle.

It wasn't so easy to find here. She loved this blade, my Tanechka. So dangerous with the *pika*.

She has her hair pulled back in a ponytail, one strand curling around her face. She takes my breath away. She pushed away the rug, refusing comfort.

She would.

I cut another slice—slowly—letting her feel it, then I pass it over. "You think you're being unlike the old Tanechka by holding so fiercely to the nun identity. What you don't understand, Tanechka, is that you have always been fierce like this. You had such a strong code of honor. We all did, but you were different. The most fierce. The most loyal."

"You won't change my mind," she says.

I hand her another slice. She loved a sweet pear.

I act cool. As if I know she'll be herself again. I slice again.

"I wanted to kill your father for the monster he was when you were growing up. So many times I wanted to kill him. But you wouldn't let me. 'He is my father,' you'd say. 'He does the best he can.'" I snort. "I wanted to gut him like a junk fish."

She regards her pear slice thoughtfully. Does she remember anything at all from then?

I take a slice for myself. "We had opposite childhoods in many ways. You had a bad father who hung onto you as if his life depended on it. You'd have been better off in an orphanage. Whereas I was in the orphanage, and I wanted a family. I'd be sent to these beautiful homes for a test, but they'd always send me back. A defective boy."

I say it casually, hating that it hurts still. I was so alone until her.

I slice off another, hand it to her.

"I'm sorry," she says.

"It's nothing." I study her pale freckles in the firelight. Her freckles are still the same. Her freckles make me feel less alone.

"It must've hurt, to be sent back."

I shrug. "I'd get a few nice meals out of it, at least. Sleep in a nice bed." Why did I start on this? Going to the family so full of hope, only to be thrown away.

That rejection was the worst kind of ache.

I find her watching me. I wipe the blade and retract it. Then I flick it out. Does she remember the sound? The *pika* was second nature to us.

The best thing about a nice sharp blade is that you don't have to cut with it; you just have to touch the person with it. The blade does the cutting for you.

"Yuri was adopted out for almost three years. He got nearly three years with a family before they sent him back. Yuri has more impulse control."

"Somebody with more impulse control than you? How is it possible?"

I look over and she's smiling.

She made a joke. Tanechka never made jokes.

"I know, right? I was so crazy back then. I'd get things into my head, and I'd burn. Like a matchstick, with my head on fire, burning with anger." It's how I felt when I thought she'd betrayed me. "I would feel as if my head was on fire."

"Do you think you're like that because you were in the room when your parents were killed?"

"Doesn't matter either way."

She contemplates the fire with sad, faraway eyes. Then, "You shouldn't be ashamed to feel deeply. You call it impulse control, but maybe you simply feel things more."

"You shouldn't make excuses for me."

"You were a boy desperate to be loved. And then I came along, and I loved you. But then I left you, didn't I?"

I concentrate on cutting the next slice, but my heart is cracking.

"You thought I was dead. It must have hurt."

I push the blade into the juicy meat of the fruit, but she's the one slicing into me. It's true—everything in my world changed when I met Tanechka. She showed somebody could love me.

And then she betrayed me, betrayed the gang. Or seemed to.

I felt so wild when I thought she'd turned traitor. A bull with arrows stuck into him.

And I killed her.

My pulse races, thinking about what Aleksio said. That I should tell the nun before I fuck her.

"I've killed many people," I say. "Some slowly and painfully. Some I tortured. I don't concern myself with hurt and love."

"I think you love your brothers. I think having a family means the world to you."

"Don't play nun with me. You won't like the result."

"You should've seen your eyes when Aleksio called you brother. You're a man who feels deeply. You want to be loved. To be forgiven. You want to be good, and you can be good."

My blood races. "Is there nothing you won't spin fairy tales about?" I grab her hair and yank her up to me. I feel insane. "Look at me. Look!"

She looks into my eyes.

"I'm not a man who feels deeply. I'm not a good man."

"I won't accept that."

"No?" I twist her hair harder. I bring her face close to mine. "No?"

Electricity grows in the space between our lips. My skin feels too tight on my body.

"You can be good," she gasps. "I know it."

I kiss her—roughly. The way she used to like. I pull her up against me, up against my cock. I nestle in my cock where I know she can feel it.

She gasps as I slide her against me, moving her ever so slightly. I often did this when she felt angry—I kissed and manhandled her, cock notched between her legs, until she softened. She didn't like when I was nice.

Don't give me smiley sex, she'd say.

"I'm not a good man, Tanechka," I say into the kiss.

She presses her hand to my chest.

"I'm the man who'll make you wet whether you like it or not," I whisper, hot into her ear. "I'm the man who'll shove apart your legs and destroy you—with just the tip of my tongue."

"Don't be a brute," she says.

"You think I'm being brutal with you? When I get brutal with you, you'll know it. You'll know it because you'll be screaming my name, begging for more."

I kiss her neck, now, merciless with my teeth. I want to mark her.

"Every curve, every breath, every nook, all of you is mine."

She hisses out a breath.

"You're feeling it now, aren't you?"

She doesn't answer, but she's soft to me now. I pull away, pull us apart.

I stare into her eyes. "I'm the man who will keep you from your god until you remember you're a devil."

With that, I turn and leave.

CHAPTER SEVENTEEN

Viktor

I spend the next day at Konstantin's with Aleksio, Yuri, and Tito.

We focus on our many operations—the brothel pipeline, the money-laundering robbery. These things we can affect.

But when I think of Tanechka trapped inside that nun, I feel helpless.

And when I think of that clerk behind a desk somewhere keeping us from the information that will lead us to Kiro, my face feels hot.

It's a good thing I don't know this desk clerk's name. But I tell myself, *Leave him alone. We're protecting Kiro by moving under the radar.*

I don't truly believe it.

I bring the old man a quilt to put over his legs, and I push him outside to feed his ducks. He gets cold. He wears an old man's hat over his bald head. "She'll remember who she is soon," I say. "I'm surrounding her with her favorite foods. Her poetry books. Clothes."

The old man throws bread. The ducks come, quacking. "It's only been a few days, Viktor. Give it time."

That's whey they all say. They don't get what it's like to have what you want most in the world in front of you and you've can't have it. Like a mirage in the desert.

"They sound like they're complaining," I say.

"Ducks. Whadya gonna do." He throws out more bread with the unsteady hands of an old man. "Maybe she needs to feel like you understand her," he says. "You bring her poetry the old Tanechka liked. What about the Bible? Why not bring her the Bible and ask her to read you her favorite part."

"I will not encourage her delusion."

"When you oppose things, you give them power—you understand that, right?"

I frown. Konstantin is a great strategist, but I don't care for this advice. "In Russia, some crazy people think they're Stalin. We'd never think to cure them by playing along."

"It's a little different, becoming a nun. Don't you think?" This he says in a voice like I'm a child.

"The old Tanechka would hate this nun."

I stop at a different Russian bakery on my way back. The Russian *Mafiya* guys here tell me it's the best, where all of their wives go. They have many lemon things for Tanechka.

I choose a selection of lemon jellies shaped like stars and lemon wedges, then I pick up a bottle of pink champagne. Tanechka would drink pink champagne like soda. Such a sweet tooth.

At home, I set the bakery bag on the counter and loosen my tie. Pityr comes up and tells me she's been quiet, except to ask for a Bible. This she is not allowed to have— I don't care what Konstantin suggests. She gets only her favorite volume of poems by Anatoly Vartov.

I take a belt of vodka, then I grab the champagne bottle, two glasses, the bag, and the rest of it, and I trudge upstairs.

I stop at the doorway. She's lying in front of the fire wearing an oversized white button-down shirt.

My shirt.

I suck in a breath, imagining the scent of it on her skin.

She wears the black jeans still—she has no choice, being that she's chained by her leg to the radiator.

She knows I'm here, but she ignores me.

I stroll in as casually as I can. I set down the bottle and the glasses.

Did she change into the shirt to be closer to me? Or is it because it's the least form-fitting thing in her closet?

Either way, I love her in it.

I take off my suit jacket and holster and set them on the bed. The gun I set on a small chest well out of her reach.

"Come here." I spread the rug back out.

She refuses to move from her place on the hard floor.

"Fine. I'll pick you up and put the rug under you and set you down on it. And if you kick it away again, I'll repeat. I'll spend all day doing it if I have to. I'll enjoy it. You'll enjoy it, too, I think."

She glares and stands up. I put out the rug. She sits on it with distaste. I open the bottle.

"No, thank you."

I pour two glasses anyway. I always have perfect control over my emotions in the field, no matter the danger. Always cool. But here in this room with her in my shirt after so long, I feel nearly crazy.

I arrange the sweets and pastries on a plate. I set a colorful cloth napkin in front of her. It's an Indian-style print. Tanechka loved such prints.

"How's the hunt for your brother going?" She gazes into the fire. "Any new leads?" She knows about the fake professor's house with the cage. It was a main subject of conversation when Aleksio and the gang were over for dinner that first night.

"We're very close, *lisichka*. But we have to move slowly."

"I bet that's hard for you," she says softly.

I look up, surprised. Tanechka was never understanding like this.

"You don't like to wait," she says. "Don't ask me how I know," she jokes.

I shake my head.

"But you love him, so you're containing yourself," she adds.

"Aleksio's good at waiting," I say. "He expects me to be like he is, but I'm not."

"Sounds like he was taught patience. From what happened to him. He expects you to be patient, too, but how could you be?"

"Exactly," I say. "It's not in me to be patient." I tell her about how our investigator is pretending to be an author. I tell her about the man behind the desk who controls the filings. "A little man playing little power games."

She hasn't moved to take a treat, so I set a lemon wedge and two jelly stars on a small plate. The lemon wedge has a sugared lemon on the top of it. She always used to pick the top it off and eat it first.

"A little man behind a desk stops you." She turns the plate clockwise, but doesn't touch the treats. "You wish you could beat it out of him."

"So badly." I kick off my shiny dress shoes and sit next to her, letting my toes warm by the fire. "But this head start is ours to exploit. We can't draw attention to ourselves, or we might squander it."

She nods. It's nice to have one person understand, even if it is the nun.

She takes her lemon wedge and looks at the top of it.

"Bloody Lazarus's organization gains in power every day," I continue. "They outnumber us by hundreds of men. We have money now, yes, but they have the empire and the connections our father built. They have strong warriors who are good at working together. If they knew where our poor *bratik* was, they could swoop in and take him out from under us. They could pluck him from a supermax prison with a word."

She picks the sugared lemon off the fluffy pastry. Only half comes up, but she puts it in her mouth.

My heart soars. She did it.

She chews with concentration. I can tell she likes it. Tanechka loves food. Back when we were together, she had more meat on her bones than this nun. Better for fighting, better for fucking.

Sometimes I couldn't believe she was mine.

"Drink your champagne," I say, taking a sip from my own glass, though it's not my kind of drink.

"I really would rather have water. Or tea."

"Jesus lets you drink wine, doesn't he?"

She stares at the fire. "It's not about that."

"You'll drink it, Tanechka, or I'll climb on top of you and press your hands above your head and dribble it into your mouth little by little."

"I'll close my lips."

"You think I can't get around that?"

In truth, I probably can't, but she doesn't know. There are some advantages to her lack of memory.

"I'll stretch out warm on top of you and make you drink, little by little," I say. "Maybe I'll tie your hands. You always loved that." I take a sip. "It's a wasteful way to drink champagne, but very erotic."

She eyes her glass. If only I could get her to take a sip.

"You'll enjoy the way I make you drink it," I say. "I'll move on top of you in a way that you'll find very pleasurable."

She takes up her glass, finally—and sips.

She holds it in front of her face, regarding it with just a tinge of wonder. Staring at the bubbles. Pink champagne. An old friend.

I take a lemon wedge and break off part. "You first had this champagne in Hotel National off Red Square. I wore my best suit—the sort to fool people who see such things. We knew how to blend, you and I. You wore a pink skirt suit—you called it your Taylor Swift outfit. You had a picture of her, and you'd style your hair like hers when we would go out pretending to be American newlyweds, our favorite cover."

I stare at the bubbles in my own glass, remembering.

"The time you first tasted this, we were in the hotel bar hoping to pick up a trail on somebody. We wore wedding rings and everything. We had the look right, but we didn't know what American newlyweds would drink." I fight to keep my face neutral as she sips again. "We knew that vodka would give us away as Russians. 'What would Taylor Swift drink?' you whispered to me. You ordered pink champagne to go with your outfit. I had a Manhattan."

She's silent for a while. Then, "Did you pick Manhattan for its name?"

"Of course," I say. "But it was wrong. Too sweet. A cherry in it. Not right."

Again she sips. Faraway eyes.

"You're a million times more beautiful than Taylor Swift."

She frowns. "Were we there to kill somebody?"

"Just scare," I say. "We followed them up to their room and did a push-in."

"We hurt them?"

I pause. "There were four others in the room we didn't expect."

"What happened?"

"We handled them."

"Six against two?"

"Numbers like that were never a problem for us." I keep my eyes on the fire as she sips again. "Remember that colorful cube I gave you at the picnic yesterday?"

She says nothing.

"A Rubik's Cube." I swirl the liquid in the glass. "We used to love them. We each had one. We'd do them side by side, up on the Borodinsky Bridge. We'd race. We came to see scenarios as Rubik's Cubes—planes of action moving this way and that. Our thinking was very aligned in this way. We could hold even a large group when we went at it like we would go at a Rubik's Cube. Five men and a woman in a hotel room. That was nothing to us."

"Did we hurt them?"

"Just one. Not badly."

She hurt one, actually. She dislocated his shoulder while I held the others at gunpoint. That was always a bit of icing on the Tanechka cake, to have the small, pretty girl do the hurting. "They were very bad people," I say. "Worse than us. We were there to deliver a message."

The story troubles her. She drinks some more.

"Just a message," I say.

"Great."

"Afterwards we walked through the square, window-shopping, pretending to be these newlyweds still."

"You can't keep me chained up."

"Maybe I like you chained up." I take the volume of Vartov from the table. "I understand you have requested the Bible to read."

She takes another lemon wedge.

"Too bad." I open to "Cages." "This poem, you loved it so much."

She shakes her head. "This will not work."

"You'd think of this poem when terrible things happened to you. So many people, when they have terrible things happen to them, they become small. Not you. You became fiercer. More loving. This poem, it spoke to your heart. It's about a man in prison, but he's able to see beauty. His heart's free, even if he isn't. You would read this poem over and over, and you'd weep." I run my finger over the Cyrillic letters, so much more elegant than English lettering.

She swirls her champagne, watching the play of light, mesmerized. It is nearly gone.

"Americans have such a different relationship with art," I say, leaving her to her champagne. "You haven't been here long, but you'll see. They're like bees, going from one thing to another. Not like us Russians, standing in front of one picture at the museum for hours, wild with feeling. We could live a whole lifetime caught in the spell of one painting. One beautiful poem." Out the corner of my eye I see her drink again. "'*Cages*' is your heart's poem."

She really was obsessed with this poem. Tanechka was more obsessive than I ever was.

Discreetly I refill her glass, and then I begin to read the poem in the original Russian, speaking her favorite lines slowly and with feeling. It's a long poem—many pages.

"So sad and beautiful," she says when I pause partway in.

She's softening to me—I can feel it. I scoot back to sit against the end of the bed. I reach out. "Come."

She stays put.

"I should make you? You think I won't? Comply with me, Tanechka, or I'll *make* you comply."

She deliberates, then comes and sits next to me on the floor against the end of the bed. I read on. The poem is melancholy. I pause and lean over to her. I speak into her hair. "You liked me to read it to you over and over."

"I did?"

"Yes."

"Over and over?" she asks. "Just like that?"

I bite back a smile. She'd sometimes do this—ask questions she knew the answer to, especially when drunk. "Over and over." She also liked me to repeat things as though I was certain of them, like strong arms around her.

I read more. I feel her rise and fall with the words. After a long silence, she says, "It makes me feel lost and lonely."

"I'm here," I say.

She sighs.

"Come." I reach around and nudge her head toward my shoulder. Miraculously, she complies, leaning her head on my shoulder.

I'm making her want me.

I begin again to read, trying to conceal my excitement.

"You would destroy my dream to be pure," she mumbles between stanzas. "More." She holds the glass out for me to fill. My heart pounds.

I fill it full of pink champagne and read on.

CHAPTER EIGHTEEN

Tanechka

I stare at Viktor's hands, so strong and sinewy, knuckles rough with life, but he cradles the fragile book.

Watching him cradle the book does something strange to me.

I focus on the poem. The poet lives his life in a prison cell, but when he sees beauty outside, he's not sad anymore.

The poem twists me inside.

I finish the drink. Bubbles and candy. I put down my glass wishing for more. I look over at the icon of Jesus and try to remember the way the light shone out from his eyes and the way it lit the faces of the goats.

Viktor transfers the book to one hand and stretches his free hand around my shoulder, pulling me closer. I shouldn't allow it, but I feel so tired and lonely, and I think I'll just rest a bit before fighting him again.

A truce.

I shouldn't enjoy it.

He pulls the band from my hair and makes it fall out. He takes a ribbon of my hair between his fingers, smoothing his thumb up and down.

I resist the impulse to turn my face to his hand and kiss it. He knows too many things about me that I don't know.

"*Lisichka?*"

"I don't remember," I tell him sadly. "It makes me feel lost not to remember this poem."

"I remember for both of us."

"That's trouble, I think."

"Never trouble, Tanechka."

I smile. I like the cozy fire. I like the bubbles.

"I don't want to be a bad person," I say. "The kind to hurt people and kill people."

"You're not a bad person," he snarls. "You were never a bad person, okay? Never. And any *kozel* who would dare to suggest it—"

He stops. Because it's me who suggested it.

"I'm sorry. I never let anyone say anything bad about you, that's all, and you shouldn't, either. You hurt people, and you saved people. You loved fiercely and wildly. You and Mischa and Yuri and the group of us, we were a family. We would die for each other."

Something in his voice catches.

"We would die for each other, and we'd want to die if we ever hurt each other," he adds.

I feel this surge of warmth for him. It's usually too much for me to look at him. But now, with my senses bright with bubbles, I like it.

So many nice things about Viktor.

His neat, close-cropped hair, as forceful and intense as he is. His rough, musky smell. I loved the way he shed his stark black jacket. And his white shirt, open at the collar, tie loose; this feels familiar, like so many things about him. The way his strong, corded neck rises from his collar.

I think of his chest under there, hard and scarred.

Quickly I look down. "Why can't you just let me be good?"

"I'll let you be good when you stop thinking you're bad." His gaze falls to my chest, then back up. "You wear my shirt."

I put on his shirt because all of the clothes he gave me are tight, but I see it was a mistake.

I feel like I'm drifting. I'm somebody else in these clothes. And the poem made me feel emotional.

He kisses my cheek. His touch is a familiar anchor.

He kisses my forehead.

I straighten away from him. "Don't."

"Fine." He takes his hand away. He curls his fingers around the corners of the book, cradling it once more. "I'll love you from here."

"Tell me more," I say.

"About what?"

"Anything." His voice is like old leather, pleasing and soft and strong. I just want to hear his voice, really.

"You loved it when I'd hold your wrists above your head," he says.

I jerk to attention. "No, not like that. I wouldn't like that, I think."

"You would. You'd love it when I'd pin your wrists to the wall or to the cool, soft bed and hold you immobile."

My face grows red. Is he right?

"I'd put my tongue into your ear. I'd lick the inside of your ear. You loved it. You said it felt like sliding through the universe. Like you were sliding in space. And then you would beg for my cock."

I swallow. "I don't believe you." Except I do—the suggestion of it glitters like dark gems in my mind.

"We had a game where I would tie you up naked—"

"These games again."

"You liked to be tied. It made you feel everything more intensely."

My pulse races. I want to hear more.

"I would tie you up naked on the bed, and you'd close your eyes, and I'd kiss you on different parts of your body. You wouldn't know where to expect the next kiss."

"That's not the game you told me before."

"It's a different one. The empty space game."

I snort. "A silly name."

"It wasn't silly." His voice is a velvet ribbon against my skin. "You'd try to feel where I was about to kiss you before my lips touched your skin. You had to feel me in the empty space between my lips and your skin."

I look away.

"When you felt me near, you'd open your eyes and look right at me. You had to catch me before I kissed you."

"Hmm."

"A game of negative space. We had many ideas about empty space, negative space, you and I. It was a *thing* for us, as they put it here. We'd sometimes spar with one of us blindfolded, using a stick for a knife. Feeling the other beyond your skin. You were a master of negative space in battle."

I sip from my glass, just for something to do.

"When you were tied and naked, you'd say that the air would tremble above the place where I was about to kiss."

A sweet feeling slides through me as I picture this. It's wrong to be attracted to this killer.

"But sometimes I'd win," he continues. "I'd sneak in a kiss." He slides his hands around the back of my neck, up to my hair. "I could always sneak under your defenses, *lisichka*."

He grips my hair, keeping my face turned to his, like a rider directing a horse.

"You're making it up," I say breathlessly.

He leans in to my ear. My heart pounds. He whispers, warm and low, "You liked me to grip your hair."

Warmth blooms inside me. That sort of wanting belongs to another life.

His lips are close to my ear. "*Pomnish*? Do you remember?" His words go through me like electricity, warm and good. He tightens his hold on my hair.

I want him to whisper something more. My heart hammers as I wait for him to show me that he has me. I'm dangerously far from Jesus now. I can barely remember the light that came from his eyes. "Let me go."

He lets go. He takes the glass from my hands. I allow it.

I feel cold now—nothing in my hand. Viktor out of my space. Cold. Lost. I hate it.

I hate being cold.

But then he turns back, and the look in his eye warms me.

"Viktor," I say.

He puts his hands over my eyes, covering them. "Where am I?" he whispers.

I snort. "What do you mean, where are you? You're right here."

"That's not what I mean," he says. "Stay still, okay?"

I wait. I feel a tickle on my cheek.

Shivers dance over my skin as some buried part of me thrills to attention. This is the game where I have to feel him before he has a chance to kiss me.

He's playing the game.

"My cheek."

"See? You still remember. Again."

"Don't bother. I'll win."

"No, you won't."

A tickle of aliveness on my cheek. "Cheek. Again. You think I'm stupid."

The tickle goes away.

"One more try," he says.

"Fine." I wait.

Nothing happens, aside from my heart pounding madly in my chest. The waiting is so tense that I laugh. It seems to last forever, the waiting.

Warmth on my neck.

"Neck," I breathe.

Warm lips press my skin.

I hiss out a breath. "It's not fair. You can't kiss me after I caught you."

"Okay," he whispers, pulling away. "Another," he says. "Feel me, little fox."

I breathe in. He's not touching me except for where his hand covers my eyes, but I feel him with every sense. I feel him stir the air around my body. I smell his sweat, and I see him strong and savage in my mind's eye.

And then the space between our lips comes alive.

"*Guby*," I whisper in the moment before he takes my lips in a warm kiss. A single kiss, there and gone.

But I feel him hovering there. He sucks in a breath, as if to breathe me in.

"Again," I say.

He kisses me roughly. This kiss feels ancient and familiar, and suddenly I'm not lost.

I slide my hands over his smooth hair. I grab it and pull. "*Yeshche*," I say into the kiss. *More.*

I need more.

The need comes from somewhere distant. From the moon, from the pink bubbles in my glass. I set my hand over his. "But keep your hand over my eyes."

"No." He yanks his hand from my eyes. "I don't want you to pretend it's not me. I need you to see me. To know it's me." He slides a hand over my hair, smoothing it down. "You liked it when I had clothes on and you did not."

I shiver, remembering how aroused I'd felt the night he touched my bare skin, telling me about my scars, the night he ripped my tunic.

"Sometimes you wanted me to heartlessly use you."

My eyes travel over his hard arms, corded with muscle. "That's not that kind of woman I am now."

"I'd play a mental trick on myself where I would imagine another man had tried to move in on you. The thought of it would make me feel wild. I'd press your hands over your head and fuck your brains out and make you mine again. You liked when I took you wild."

Every nerve ending on my skin comes alive at the thought of him pushing me down and taking me like that.

"Our *bratva* superiors would sometimes send us on stake outs. We'd have to pose as strangers in public places. I had to pretend not to know you. I enjoyed that because I'd see you from the eyes of a stranger, and I'd have to treat you coolly, but inside my hunger for you would rage." He smiles at the memory. "You'd always taunt me a little bit. You loved anytime I played the dark stranger. When we'd finally be off the job, we'd pretend we were still strangers and be fucking sometimes before we hit the car. In an alley, often. We'd talk to each other in our stranger roles. I would push you up against a wall and take you wild like a stranger."

I look away, my mind a maelstrom. I'm drunk on the sound of his voice and his dark stories.

"You liked a little pressure right on your neck—"

"No, I wouldn't—I couldn't."

"Not choking. Just a little...like this. Can I?"

"Yes."

He presses his huge hand to my neck, his palm rough and warm on my tender skin. He pushes my head backwards to the end of the bed and holds me there. "Claiming pressure. Exactly like that."

My sex throbs. My pulse bangs against his fingers.

"Just enough to let you know you're mine. To let you know I'll take you in whatever way I wish."

I should push his hand away, but I don't. Instead, I say, "Like that?"

"Just like that."

"*Just* like that?"

He grins. He removes his hand from my neck and lifts me. My leg chains clank as he lays me down on the rug. He kneels over me. "You liked it just like that."

His dark eyes flash in the firelight as he threads his fingers into mine, our hands forming two fists.

His tie hangs loose, sliding against the side of my neck as he presses my hands over my head and down onto the thick shag rug.

The rough fur of the rug abrades the backs of my hands. He holds me still like that, dark eyes fierce above me, inky lashes flashing in the firelight.

His eyes drift to where my pulse throbs in my neck. He sees everything.

"Viktor," I say.

"What, *lisichka?*"

"I'm too far away." I don't know whether I mean from him or from Jesus.

"I have you." He kneels over me, trapping my legs with his feet and knees now, while he holds my hands in place over my head. "You always felt safe when you were trapped like this." He gazes down into my eyes. "Again?"

I narrow my eyes.

"Where am I now?"

The game. But he's not covering my eyes this time. I gasp as he lowers himself to me. He presses himself down between my legs, pressing his hard ridge to my sex. I roll my hips up to meet the feeling. It's so good.

"Where am I?"

"You're not playing right," I pant.

He transfers my hands to one hand, still capturing them, and then he takes my chin in his hand and kisses me.

I kiss him back, moving under him, taking more of his ridge with my body. I think I've travelled somewhere.

He presses his hand onto my breast, then. "This shirt. You kill me with this shirt and nothing underneath. You kill me." His voice sounds strange.

He kisses my neck and starts to unbutton my shirt. *His* shirt. He kisses every new patch of skin that he bares to the air. One button, then another button, more skin, another kiss. He finds my tattoo and kisses it. He'll have my shirt open soon.

I lock my legs around his. The push of his body overwhelms me.

"Tanechka," he whispers, pressing his hand to my belly. "I have you." He slides his hand up and down me, creating sweet, warm friction as he kisses my neck.

"More," I say, desperate.

He presses his hand down on my stomach. "Like this?"

"Yes."

"I have you, *lisichka.*"

I rock my hips, body craving for him to go lower. He unbuttons my jeans and yanks down the zipper.

Cool air hits the tender skin below my belly.

He presses his hand under my panties, finding the slick wetness between my legs. He just presses there.

I gasp from the feeling.

And then he begins to move his fingers. Gently, slowly, as his breath heats my ear.

"*Yeshche*," I say. "More."

He invades the seam between my legs with confidence. Arrogance, even.

His finger feels impossibly thick and blunt.

"I'll never deserve you, but I'll always take you," he grates out. He pushes my knees farther apart and slides his finger up and down, stroking up and down. His slow, steady strokes are dark magic.

My eyes drift closed, picturing his capable hand at my sex.

"Look at me," he whispers as he roams two fingers over my sex, over swollen skin full of feeling.

I keep my eyes shut. Viktor is my anchor. But he's also the man pulling me out to sea.

"Come back to me," he growls. "You have to see me."

I open my eyes.

"There you are." He kisses me as he strokes me. He invades my mouth with his tongue into my mouth as he lengthens his stroke.

I'm sucking his tongue. Something inside me knows to do this.

He's stroking me harder.

I suck his tongue harder as a signal for more.

He groans and complies. It's just right.

With his other hand he presses my hands back to the carpet with renewed force. His domination gives me a helpless feeling that I love.

I'm a creature living on his touch like a vine living on air.

I release his tongue, and he growls and nips my lip, then he sucks it, sharply, painfully.

So good.

A glittery, floaty sensation slides through me. The rawness inside me is like a waterfall of tears.

He grunts as he trails his tongue up my cheek and deep into my ear. I hiss out a breath.

Every thought leaves me.

Like sliding through the universe. He told me that's how it would feel.

It feels better than that.

He invades me and sets me spinning through the stars. His massive fingers stoke a fire between my legs.

"Tanechka," he breathes, low and rough, pressing my hands above my head, reminding me that I'm safe.

The feeling explodes over me, takes me over, carries me. I spin on, stars in my mind. I cry out, exploding with sensation.

A wilderness of stars.

It's only after the feeling leaves me that I realize the horror of what I've done. I push him away and scramble back, buttoning my pants, pulling his shirt around me, sitting against the end of the bed.

I'm shaking. I feel crazy.

"*Lisichka.*"

"Don't call me that!"

He smiles.

I feel hot and crazy. A puppet out of control.

And suddenly I'm on top of him. My hands are around his throat, one thumb pressed against the side of a little bone in there.

I have only to snap that bone.

CHAPTER NINETEEN

Viktor

I look into her angry blue eyes, into the heat of her hate.

She's a gorgeous angel of vengeance, skin flushed, hair wild.

She trembles as she grips my neck.

"Tanechka," I say. "Take what you need."

She narrows her eyes. "You *want* me to kill you?"

My heart pounds.

She begins to squeeze. She could crush the guilt and shame from me with one single squeeze. "You'd die to take me from Jesus? Is that it?"

Okay, she's still the nun.

A moment later, she eases off. She stands up, glowering. "No matter what you've done, you're lovable. You are worthy of God's love."

"Stop talking about God!"

"God knows your heart, and he loves you. He knows you, and he still loves you."

I surge to my feet and slam my fist into the wall. The skin breaks, but I don't care. "Stop talking about God!"

I slam my fist in again and again.

"I don't want your stupid God's love." Plaster breaks around my knuckles, gouges my skin. "I don't want your stupid prayers!"

"Stop, Viktor!"

I keep on. I'm out of her reach. She can't stop me.

I picture her face the day I shoved her into Dariali Gorge. The way she pleaded with me. The way she clung to me. *Predatel*, I called her.

I was nineteen with my hair on fire. So in love with her that I was beyond reach.

And I killed her.

I punch the wall again and again. My fist is wet with blood, the pain more and more intense.

I didn't believe in her like I should've. I didn't understand she was operating as a double agent to save her mother. All we knew was that she'd given secrets to the enemy. Kissed their leader. I went crazy when I saw the photos.

Again and again I hit the wall.

It was only later that we put it together. We found a notebook where she'd worked it all out, and I could see the Rubik's Cube thinking in it.

Too late.

The hole in the wall grows red with my blood.

"Viktor!"

"Don't say my name like you know me."

That's when the shot rips out, like an explosion in the wall to my right. I still and turn, ears ringing, pulse racing.

She has my Glock. The rug is bunched up on the floor. Did she use the rug to pull the gun to her? "Get over here," she growls.

My throbbing fist is warm with blood. "Tanechka?"

She gestures with the gun at a spot on the floor in front of her. "Now."

She's back. Again she gestures at the floor.

I fall to my knees in front of her. "I'd die a million times to take it back—"

"Quiet," she growls.

Tanechka!

I never thought I'd see her again. Once more she gestures with the gun. "Lie down. Face-down on the floor."

Cold shivers go over me. She means to shoot me execution style.

It's only right.

Except I want to die looking at her. I want to look at her as I breathe my last breath, as the pain melts away.

"Down! Do it!"

I swallow. This is what I've earned, then. To die at her hands, face shoved into the bearskin rug.

I suck in a breath and lay myself in front of her, fingers knit behind my neck. I breathe into the rough fur.

"I'm not afraid," I say. "Make me suffer as I made you suffer. End this. I've waited so long." My pain will be washed clean by the only person who can wash it.

She kicks me. "Lie on your side."

I turn to my side. Whatever way she wants it.

She stands over me. I look at her stocking feet. The ragged ends of the jeans. "Eyes shut," she commands.

I shut my eyes. I hear a soft rustling sound above me. She's on the rug behind me.

I picture her face. She'll be the last thing I think of.

There's a tickle on the back of my head.

A hand drapes over my arm.

She stretches her body out behind mine. She presses a kiss to the back of my neck.

And holds me.

"What are you doing?"

"Shh," she says, pulling me tighter. "Shh."

CHAPTER TWENTY

Lazarus

I'm sitting in my Mercedes on a street near Ping Tom Park.

It's a place I like to go and think, but right now I'm on a phone consultation with Valerie. She's encouraging me to personally visit Dmitri, leader of the American Russians.

"Visit my enemy…" I say. "Maybe I should bring him a little gift, too. But what do you bring the man who wants your head on a platter? Fruitcake doesn't seem quite right."

She laughs. She thinks I'm using it as a figure of speech.

I told her that I'm in a rivalry with a Russian accounting firm. I told her how competition for some business got out of hand, right when I don't need the extra headache.

"Your people stepped over a line," she says.

"That's one way of putting it." I say.

Another—more accurate—way of putting it would be that two of my guys got wasted on meth and shot some Russian mob soldiers. Managing criminals isn't as easy as it might appear. A lot of them are hotheads and addicts.

"Maybe I could bring him their heads on platters."

"Is that what he really wants, though?" She thinks I don't mean that literally, either. "What are Dmitri's business objectives?"

"Operational expansion," I say. "Conservation of human resources." This is how Valerie and I talk. My guys would fall off their chairs if they heard us.

"What I'm getting at is, if you want to prevent more sniping between your firms, look at it from his point of view. Imagine you weren't rivals. What becomes possible then? Who are you without this rivalry? What's on both of your business bucket lists? What makes you both look good in the eyes of the rank and file? Is there any sort of joint venture you could undertake? Or a pooling of resources to catch a large account that you both want? Think out of the box here, Lazarus. Maybe you collaborate to put on a charity event for a cause you both believe in and the Russian firm name is at the top. You'll make him look good."

Making people look good is one of Valerie's go-to strategies.

"He's gonna have some significant trust issues," I say.

"Then overcome them, Lazarus. When was the last time you and Dmitri met face to face?"

Never, I tell her. No, not even at an *industry function*.

She's surprised. "The first step is a meeting. Humanize yourself to him. Invite him to dinner."

"Just the two of us?"

"Two guys. Who probably have very much in common."

It's an interesting idea. Insane, but interesting.

I imagine sitting down with Dmitri in an out-of-the-way restaurant. Something neutral—not Agronika, the Black Lion club. Not one of the Russki places, either. There would need to be guarantees of safety.

"I don't know. I don't want him to think I'm fearful of his retaliation. Going to him on my knees. Kissing his ass."

"In judo, a fighter uses his opponent's energy against him. When the opponent pushes, you pull. Your Russian rival is in pushing mode. Instead of pushing back, why not surprise him? Why not find a way to pull him close? You let him know you didn't sanction that action that your employees took. You're disciplining them, right?"

"They won't misbehave again."

"Good. Let him know the steps you've taken toward bringing your team back under control. Then move forward—find some point of agreement and build."

"It's...out of the ordinary."

"Guess what, Lazarus. You're in control now. You get to decide what's ordinary now."

CHAPTER TWENTY-ONE

Viktor

When I open my eyes again, it's dawn, my phone's ringing from somewhere, and Tanechka's still a nun.

Her arm is still around me. It's nice, I suppose, but it's not for me. It can never be for me.

Gently, I remove her arm and settle her on her back, gazing down at her sleeping form. Nobody ever held me like that. Nobody ever told me I was worthy—not even the old Tanechka.

The old Tanechka wouldn't say that.

I sit on the end of the bed and check my phone to see who called.

Telling me I'm worthy. A nun probably says it to everybody.

The call was from Yuri. I call back. It is not good news. Some of Bloody Lazarus's guys ambushed some of our

American Russian friends. We have to help them avenge it.

It will be dangerous and bloody, but they're important allies, and to have an ally, you must be an ally.

Aleksio is busy investigating a Kiro lead.

It's up to me.

"I'll be outside my door, *brat.*"

I button up my shirt, wincing at the pain. My hands are caked with dried blood. Nothing broken, I think.

Tanechka sleeps.

I buckle my holster and put on my suit jacket. I kneel over her and smooth a stray lock of hair from her forehead.

She mumbles sleepily. Opens her eyes.

I stand up and fasten my cufflinks, looking down, affecting a cold demeanor. "I'm going out. To kill some men. You will pray for me?" I say it mockingly.

"Viktor," she says sadly.

I head downstairs and bandage my hand. I swallow pain relievers with a swig of vodka. Two minutes later I'm outside with my case. Yuri roars up in his black Mustang. I swing in.

"What the fuck?" he says.

The car screams around a corner.

"What?"

"You hand. What did you do?"

I flex it. "Nothing broken." The pain relievers should kick in soon. I would've taken something stronger if I didn't need my aim. "I punched a wall."

"You can shoot still, right?"

"Yeah." I change the subject, ask about the ambush. Yuri and some of the American Russians have identified the man as one of Lazarus's. "They want a full-scale war on Lazarus—now," Yuri says.

"A full-scale war is a poor use of our resources."

"You sound like old Konstantin."

"Konstantin is smart."

"They don't want to wait," Yuri says. "They're scared."

"So impatient." A full war puts Bloody Lazarus's organization into the shell of battle mode. It makes them hard to hurt in the deep way we need to hurt them. "We'll take out the hitters. That should satisfy them until we attack Lazarus's money-laundering op. When they see the cash they get from that, they'll be glad we waited."

Yuri doesn't like it. "That would go over better if Aleksio hadn't missed that meeting."

"They're our brothers. They'll understand."

"They're more American than Russian," he says. "They make tacos out of shuba, Viktor. *Shuba.*"

I wrinkle my nose.

"Your hand. Tell me."

I look down at my bandaged hand. "I thought it was her," I say. "I thought for a moment that I had Tanechka back."

"Still thinks she's a nun, huh."

"I thought she'd snapped out of it. She got my gun, and for a moment I thought she was going to shoot me—"

"You gave her a piece?"

"I didn't *give* it to her."

"Did the *nocnitsa* float through the wall and give it to her? What are you thinking?"

"Just drive."

* * *

Pityr's in the kitchen when I return. "Did you do them?"

Did we kill Lazarus's men, he means.

"They were already dead," I say. "Killed last night. Their bodies found in Bobolink Meadow. Hands and feet gone."

He narrows his eyes, confused. A Bloody Lazarus trademark. "Why would Bloody Lazarus kill his own men like that?"

"I don't know. We went to see ourselves, and it's true. Then, going back to the car, we ran into a guy from Valhalla. It looked like he recognized me from my Peter the German visit. We had to kill him."

Pityr shrugs. "He would've blown all that careful work."

I loosen my tie. "Is Tanechka awake?"

"Yes, and she asked for vodka."

I straighten. Only the old Tanechka would ask for vodka. "You gave her some?"

"I hope it's okay."

I clap a hand on his cheek. "Of course, Pityr. She can have all the vodka she wants. Anything she wants."

"Except a Bible."

"Right. Did she say anything else?"

"No. Just to bring her the bottle of vodka."

"Not even a glass?"

Pityr shakes his head. "You think she remembers?"

Maybe.

I clap him on the shoulder and turn to leave.

"Wait!" He grabs my arm. "You want backup? If she remembered, don't you want to be ready?"

"I'm always ready. Don't disturb us." I take the stairs three by three.

I hear the weeping in the hall. I burst into the bedroom. "Tanechka?"

She's curled up in front of the fire, cheeks streaked with tears, bottle in one hand, volume of poems in the other. "Is this how I would overcome the killing?"

Still the nun.

I kneel by her and try to take the book from her, but she won't let me have it.

"It's in the darkness and squalor of his cell that he most feels free," she says. "The prisoner feels such beautiful freedom and goodness because it's what he can never have again. It's how I feel now, drifting so far from the convent."

For a moment, I think about giving up on everything and taking her there. She wants it so badly.

She clutches the book and the bottle to her breast. A pale, beautiful creature, feeling so wildly.

I sit and draw her to me, holding her.

"Anyone you killed, you had to kill."

"Answer me, Viktor. Is this how I'd overcome it?"

"No, Tanechka. We would never overcome it. That was never our goal."

"What was our goal?" she asks.

I settle her against me and take the bottle from her fingers. I drink. "This poem of Vartov, it let you feel the darkness, but you knew there was something good, too. Goodness somewhere else."

She listens, a silent, deadly flower.

"When you're a killer, you have to find a way to stay human. That's a hard thing."

"How did *you* stay human?" she asks.

You, I want to say. I don't. "Best I could."

She sniffs. A soft laugh.

I drink some more. I want to be drunk like her. "Some men in our old gang would grow hard with killing. They would grow a hard crust. The kind of people where, when they walk into a restaurant, nobody wants to be near them. Not because they're scary, but because they're... *oni zhutkiy.*" I can't think of the American word for it. Maybe *yucky.*

I feel her smile.

"We didn't like to work with men like that. We preferred to work together, you and I."

"You think we were a superior class of killers?"

I twirl my finger in her hair. "I don't know. I think it is always better to feel it than to have a hard crust."

She snorts. Does she understand how like Tanechka she is being?

"I think if we didn't stay human like that, we couldn't have felt the love for each other that we did. We were hard to the world, but human to each other."

"I feel sad," she says. "I'm sorry you can't have your old Tanechka back."

"You're not so different from her," I say. "You believe in things so fiercely. You'd hang on to hope after everybody else lost their faith."

She'd hang onto grudges, too.

I hand her the bottle and she takes another drink. "I want an update on Valhalla. Are you moving on them soon?"

"Soon," I say.

"They can't wait, Viktor."

"I've told you why it can't be instantaneous."

"I don't like it."

A long silence. It's a good silence. We always could be silent together.

"You know what else is the same, *lisichka?*"

"What?" she asks.

"You always saw the sky. 'Look at that cloud, Viktor. Look at the sunset. Look at the sky, how blue, how pale it becomes at the edges.' You're still looking up. As a nun."

"Almost a nun," she says.

"As almost a nun."

I think, suddenly, that she's beautiful in her doomed desire to be a nun. She's like a fish, swimming and swimming in a tiny bowl with us other fish, imagining a beautiful ocean beyond.

Except she can never get there.

I won't let her.

CHAPTER TWENTY-TWO

Tanechka

There's blood on his shirt. I don't say anything because I don't want him to change.

I want the blood to remind me of what he is.

It doesn't work. He's too dangerous, too beautiful.

I need to get to the convent, to reconnect with my kind. There has to be a key to the iron cuff somewhere, but he knows not to bring it into my range. You never bring the keys around the prisoner. I know this the way I know you never put your hand into the fire.

Because I, too, am a killer.

I push him away and force myself to look at his bloody shirt. This is a person's blood.

He notes the direction of my gaze. With a jerk he rips off his tie and fights off his shirt like it's an octopus clinging to him. He pulls it all off himself and tosses it angrily aside revealing his muscular chest. Two rosy nipples. A smattering of dark hair leading down to his belly. So many scars. He sits back against the end of the bed.

More beautiful. More dangerous.

I snuggle up next to him. His skin is warm and smooth against my cheek. His touch nourishes me in a way that food does not.

My eyes drift closed. It's a comfort to me, the way he strokes my hair, sliding his fingers down the smooth surface of it. "It breaks me apart when you're sad, *lisichka.*"

Without thinking, I grab the bottle and drink more. More vodka. More Viktor.

The muscles of his chest shift as he takes the bottle from my fingers, takes a swig for himself. The movement feels familiar. Like old times, probably.

The bare skin above his belt looks softer than the rest. I know exactly how it would feel to place my palm there— smooth and silky warm with just a little rough. The memory is in my hand.

The memory is in my lips, too. In my face.

I say, "Back at the convent, I had a tiny room with just a bed and a desk. It was a happy life."

He holds the bottle loosely, reflecting a streak of firelight. "Tell me what you loved about it."

I tell him about the beauty of the place. I tell him how I felt so lost at first, always so angry and grieving, and the patience and love the mothers there showed me. And how brave they were in the face of the soldiers.

"I would loll in the grass in the sun while the goats grazed. They would come to me and nuzzle me. They would play."

"It sounds beautiful," he says. "So peaceful."

"You would love it. You would love the mothers there too."

"Hmm…"

I snatch the bottle from him. "You would." I drink. "The most amazing thing was when I found the icon."

He tips his chin to the shelf. "That one?"

"No, it was an old one, thought to be lost. I was on a hillock with the goats, and I saw such a sweet bright light. Like nothing you've ever seen, Viktor."

I don't know what makes me tell it. I think because it feels so natural to be with him. I tell him how the light shone from it. How the goats gathered. How it felt in my heart. How I ran back to show the mothers, and what they said.

He smooths his thumb along my cheek. I close my eyes. I want to drink him up with my body. "You were happy?"

"Yes."

"Do you want to go back?"

"I will go back. After the women are safe."

I settle my palm onto his chest, so thick and hard. I don't feel lost when I touch him. When he kissed me roughly that time, I didn't feel lost.

Turn back, I say to myself. *You are drunk.*

I say this to myself even as I slide my hand across his skin. Even as I touch his rosy nipple, puckered in a swirl of hair. He puts his hand over mine—to try to stop me?

"What do you want?" His breath has gone ragged.

"To not be lost." I slide my hand lower, fingers under his belt.

There's a long silence. He takes the bottle and drinks while I touch him. He looks so troubled.

"Help me not be lost."

He pauses a moment more, then he puts the bottle down and yanks me up to his lap, taking my mouth roughly, fitting my body to his, sending pleasure between my legs.

Before I know it, I'm on my back, and he's straddling me, looming above me.

I slide my hands up and down his hard thighs, spread over me like mighty tree trunks. He watches me carefully as he moves his hands to my collar. In one wild motion he rips my shirt in two, baring my breasts.

I laugh in surprise. He said I don't like smiley sex, but I like this.

He kisses a line down my belly to my waistband. He unbuttons my jeans and shoves them and my panties all the way down, off the ankle without the metal iron. He kisses back up my bare legs.

My heart pounds as he pauses near my sex.

I gasp as he licks me there once and again. I hiss out a breath as he spreads my legs even farther apart, licking.

I grab onto his hair as he teases me, nips me, a horrible, perfect, wonderful torture. I don't want him to stop this magic.

And he doesn't.

Even when I cry out and break apart, spinning in feeling, he keeps on. I've barely come down when he's over me, putting on a condom onto himself. He holds himself over me, one massive arm planted next to mine.

With his other he touches me, running his fingers along the underside of my forearms, gliding gently over my skin.

He makes me feel sparkles and light. "Look at me," he says.

The command makes my sex throb. I turn my gaze up to him. He is not a good man, but I want him.

He watches my face, seeming to be searching for something.

Watching me, holding me with his gaze, he brings his arm down between us and guides himself to my entrance, pressing his manhood between my legs. I feel the fat bulb of his head.

I suck in a breath, stunned by the hugeness of him. Then he thrusts inside me, filling me with his hugeness, with pain and possession.

"More," I gasp.

He fits his hand around my neck with the claiming pressure he promised.

My pulse bangs against his fingers as he fucks me. My sex pulses with electricity. It feels like magic going through me.

The squeeze is like a hypnotic command. This dangerous pressure that tells me I'm his. That he'll take me in whatever way he wishes.

"More," I gasp.

He squeezes my neck and shoves my legs further apart, spreading me open wide.

The feeling of him inside me is perfect beyond imagination.

I cry out in agony and pleasure.

CHAPTER TWENTY-THREE

Viktor

I fuck her fast and hard, spearing her. It's what she loves, to be pounded into oblivion.

"You're never lost with me, *lisichka*."

She whimpers and digs her nails into my shoulders. I growl and hold her, take her, giving her everything I am. I close my eyes as I give her everything.

On and on I go, slow and savage now. I slide against her clit. Her orgasm likes to run and hide. But I'm a lethal hunter.

"Wait," she says, breaking me from my reverie. "Wait."

I slow, surprised to see her eyes so clear and bright. Has she remembered?

"Slow," she says.

I suck in a ragged breath. We don't do slow.

"I want to feel you," she says. "*You.*"

It breaks me a little bit.

"Please."

I hesitate, but she watches my eyes so trustingly. Depending on me. I move my trembling hand from her neck to her cheek. "Like this?"

"Like that."

I close my eyes and move into her slowly. I don't know how to do it—it's too much. But I pull out and press in, loving her nakedly, shaking with every slow thrust.

If this is the end, I'll do it how she wants.

The affection in her gaze overwhelms me.

I know that I should let her go, to bring her back to the convent, the one place she had peace.

But I can't. I have to make her remember.

"So good." She arches under me, pulling me into her.

She's coming. I know it before she does. Her sex clenches around me, milking me. She cries out, pure as a bell.

I hold her, kiss her as she comes. As we come together. I hold her until the last shudder leaves her body.

I watch her face. She looks different. Is she remembering? "Tanechka?"

I can't read her expression.

"Do you remember?"

She looks at me so strangely. What does it mean?

Just then, tires squeal nearby. The sound of vehicles converging.

Danger. I grab my phone and text Yuri with a "?".

Nothing back.

A tingle runs up my spine. Is he hurt?

I pull on my clothes and my holster. "Get dressed, Tanechka. We have to leave."

She doesn't budge. She stares at the icon. "I'm so far from him now."

My heart sinks. Still the nun. "We must leave. You want me to take you out of here naked?" I shrug as if I don't care.

Downstairs a door bangs. No—it's a shoulder. People trying to get in.

"Put on your clothes!" I bound down the stairs, piece drawn. I nearly collide with Pityr coming up.

"The American Russians," he says. "They've turned on us."

"What?"

He tosses me my rifle and pushes me back up. "We're surrounded. Yuri was hit—only in the shoulder."

"Where is he?"

"Out of here. Safe."

My phone goes off. Aleksio. "I'm coming, Viktor. Hold them off."

Tanechka has pulled her clothes back on, thankfully. I throw Pityr the keys to her ankle cuff, and I run to the weapons safe. I grab two grenades and a nine and get to the window. They haven't gotten in yet. The Russians reinforced this condo—steel construction techniques. Their own cleverness foils them.

"What's going on?" Tanechka asks.

"Stay down. Close your eyes and plug your ears!" I break the window glass with the butt of the rifle. Then I crouch and pull the pin from the grenade. "Ears!" I say again.

When her ears are safely covered, I toss it and crouch.

Alarmed voices. The sound of men scrambling. The blast of a grenade shakes the floor. I straighten up and start shooting, clearing the street. Pityr takes up position on the other side, taking people out.

Sirens sound in the distance.

This is very bad. If the American Russians turned, it's Bloody Lazarus who turned them. The cops won't be interested in saving us. The cops may be interested in fighting us, too.

I take a few more shots. Fire is returned. Windows break. The beautiful nest I made for my Tanechka is going to burn.

"Aleksio has a bulletproof Hummer," I say. "He's coming."

Tanechka nods.

What would happen if I put a gun in her hand? She used to be so fierce in a fight like this. Dependable. Black cap covering the bright target of her hair. Would her body still remember?

But I've damaged her enough today. "Stay down."

I suck in a breath and rise up to shoot again. They were supposed to be our brothers, these Russians. I should've been more attentive. I should've seen this.

This is on me. And if Yuri is hurt...

More shoulders slamming the door below. A window breaks.

"The roof," I say to Pityr. "We torch this place and take the roof. The way Tanechka did. Okay? Tanechka, you ready?"

She nods, goes to the fireplace. She'll start the blaze. She knows to do this. Is she remembering?

I call Aleksio. "How far are you?"

"Two minutes," he says.

"We're going over the rooftops to Reston Ave."

"Neva Street is better," Tanechka says, as if in a trance.

"Scratch that—Neva Street," I say. "Come up the south alley." We talk tactics. I'm going to lob out another grenade. I nod at Tanechka, and she sets the bedspread on fire.

"*Davay davay davay*," Pityr calls from across the hall, wanting us to hurry. "On your call."

"You first—with Tanechka."

"No. I'll stay!"

"You first!" He doesn't like me doing the suppressing because it means I'll be the last up. It means I'll be in the most danger. But I'm his superior. He'll obey.

And this is how I best protect Tanechka—by giving her and Pityr the best cover.

"Now!"

Tanechka leads the way to the attic. The fire's spreading. I stay.

When I hear them punch out the window up there, I begin strafing, clearing the street. When I can no longer see through the smoke, I run to the hall and head up to the attic.

I cough. My eyes water. I waited too long, but I know where the window is. I climb up and out. Once on the roof, I hurl the grenade. Then I run.

I meet them hanging over the fire escape.

I cough, catching my breath. "Go!"

We climb down.

Aleksio screams up to us. Tanechka drops first—right onto the hood like a pro. Pityr goes next.

Gunfire from the corner.

Aleksio shoves open his door and starts shooting up the street. I go for it, dropping down. I feel the wind of a bullet near my leg. I'm in.

Aleksio roars off before I can close the door. The back window cracks under the impact of multiple rounds. I spin around. "Tanechka?"

"Get the fuck down!" Aleksio says.

"Tanechka?"

"I'm okay," she says, crouched.

I slide back around. "Where's Yuri?"

"With Mischa," Aleksio said. "He's fine. He was across the street when they surrounded the place. They started taking guys out and got it. Check yourself, brother."

"I'm okay," I say.

We get on a main drag out of the city. Aleksio tells me he's been trying Konstantin. No answer.

"He's okay," I say hopefully. "Probably out with his ducks." Still, it's worrisome.

There are many stoplights, some of them red. Aleksio goes through one, then another. We gun it, putting in the distance, heading for Konstantin's place.

"Listen to me—they didn't send Kiro to Stillwater prison," Aleksio says. "He was sent to Oak Park Heights. Criminally insane shit. Don't forget it."

My heart thunders for what Aleksio doesn't say. If one of us is killed, it's up to the other to get to Kiro. "We'll find him together."

"Right. Here's the thing—he was sent there but he's not listed. Maybe under an alias. We have to figure it out. That's where we are with it."

"We'll get him," I growl. "If I have to burn the place down myself."

"Maximum security. Can't go in hot."

We're heading past Lombard when red cherries light behind us.

"Fuck," Aleksio says. Chances are good that they're not after us because of our traffic violations. "Don't worry— I'm gassed up."

"Gotta get clear before the choppers come out," I say, stating the obvious.

He guns it down a main artery. That's when we see the train.

"Fuck," Pityr says.

"This is good. We can do this." Aleksio races up the frontage road, racing the thing with the cops hot on our trail.

Aleksio loves to call me a madman. He's no different.

We get almost level with the engine when we come to the crossing, a line of cars stretched out, like a wall in front of us, stretching out to our right, the train coming up on the left.

I spin around in my seat. "Hold on, *lisichka*."

I don't have to tell her. She's holding tight. Pityr's riding with a stony face. He, too, holds on.

"Here we go!" Aleksio veers left over the tracks in front of the oncoming train, barely clearing it.

The train barrels by behind us, a thundering wall of steel between the cops and us.

For now.

"We have to ditch this vehicle," Pityr says. "This Hummer is burned, burned, burned."

"Agreed."

Moments later, Aleksio pulls into a commuter parking lot. It's perfect—many cars nobody will miss for hours.

We all jump out. Pityr hotwires a Mazda. I go to Tanechka. "Are you okay?"

She looks up at me, as if she doesn't comprehend the question.

I fucked her. She's lost everything—again. Because of me.

I say nothing. There's just surviving for now. I make her get in the back with Pityr. I take the wheel with Aleksio at my side.

"What happened?" Aleksio asks quietly, tipping his head at Tanechka in the back.

She talks with Pityr in low tones.

I shake my head.

He gives me a dark look, and we set off.

"The fuck," he says after a bit.

He's not talking about Tanechka this time; he's talking about our Russian friends turning. Our best allies are gone—to the most powerful crime organization in the ten-state area…and they're all united with the cops.

"I had the money-laundering heist set up with them for tomorrow. We would've cleaned him out. It would've made us solid with the Russians."

"The Russians knew about the camera."

"Probably told Lazarus about it by now," Aleksio says. "This is on me, *brat*. I should have spent more time with Dmitri."

"It's on me, too." I nod my head back toward Tanechka. I was spending all my time with her.

"I thought they hated Lazarus,"Aleksio growls. "This is the last time we underestimate him."

"Him going after us shows he doesn't know where Kiro is," I say. "We can still find Kiro. Together the Dragusha brothers will rain fire on Bloody Lazarus. And we'll have our empire back."

At least the brothel pipeline has nearly collapsed. One more week and we can raid it.

We switch vehicles a few miles later, nabbing a nice SUV. We head south to Konstantin's quiet senior village.

Whispering trees line shady sidewalks. Low-rise brick buildings stretch for entire blocks. One unit has the door swinging open.

Konstantin's.

My heart drops.

Aleksio tears into the driveway and jams it into park. He's out of the car, running for the door before any of us can move.

I take out my Glock and twist around to Pityr and Tanechka in the back seat. Pityr has his weapon out.

Tanechka's blue eyes are wide. Not with surprise, but with looking. Observing. Waiting. "Stay here until we make sure it's clear," I say to her.

I get out of the vehicle in a haze.

Konstantin is dead. I don't need to see his body to know. I don't need to hear Aleksio's cry of rage and anguish from inside the door.

Pityr and I move in opposite directions along the fronts of the low-rise homes, covering the drives and the carefully tended grass with long, quick strides, weapons down at our thighs. We converge around the back. The ducks quack.

We head in.

The old man is on the foyer floor, a pool of blood under his cheek, gun in his hand, the back of his head blown off. Aleksio is on his knees next to him, his head on the old man's chest.

I put my hand on his shoulder. "Stay," I say. "We'll clear."

We steal through the place, clearing room by room. We find no intruders. We find no struggle.

"*Mne ochen zhal,*" Pityr says to me in the dark hall when we know the place is clear. "I'm so sorry."

"I knew him only a year. But to Aleksio, he was a father," I say. "Get Tanechka out of the driveway. And call Mira. Aleksio needs Mira with him."

I go back into the foyer to find Aleksio. He's still next to Konstantin, grasping his hand.

I kneel next to my brother and touch the old man's arm. Still warm. Three hours dead, maybe.

After a while, I pull Aleksio away from the body. It's not good to let people cling to a body. I take Aleksio in my arms and hold him with everything I have inside me, squeezing him without shame. "*Brat.*" There is nothing more to say.

"He gave me everything," Aleksio whispers hoarsely into my shoulder. "He gave up his life to save me."

"A soldier and a father." I squeeze him. This brother I love. This brave old man dead.

"He killed himself," Aleksio says. "I can't tell for sure, but the angle...his piece..." He pauses, overcome. "They came to the door, and he knew they'd hurt him to get what he knows of Kiro, of us. He killed himself rather than give anything up."

"He died protecting us."

"I closed his eyes and his mouth," Aleksio says. "He taught me that. An Albanian custom, done to stop death from coming again.

He didn't believe in the superstitions, but he wanted me to know our culture, to know the little things and the big things, like *besa*."

Besa. Honor, it means. For the crazy Albanians, *besa* is everything.

I let go of Aleksio and bend down to kiss the old man's forehead. "You believed, old man. You never stopped fighting. The strongest of us all."

Aleksio stands over me with his fist shoved into his face, as though the pain is too much.

I rise and set a hand on his shoulder.

"Sometimes I would be scared as hell just to fall asleep," Aleksio says. "Right after it happened, especially."

He doesn't have to say what "it" is. "It" is the night Aldo Nikolla and Bloody Lazarus slaughtered our parents.

"I was so full of fucking terror. This shit that would take over my body, you know? We'd live in these shitty apartments with walls like paper, him doing whatever dangerous scams he had to do to get us by, keep us under the radar. We'd have to move every week, but no matter where we went, the first thing he'd do was set up a chair at the foot of my bed or sleeping bag." He turns to Konstantin. "Remember?"

He kneels and sets a hand lightly on the old man's arm.

"Remember all the nights you slept in a chair at the foot of my bed? Did you even sleep back then?" He scrubs a hand over his face.

I set a hand on his shoulder. "He was a father."

"Sometimes when it was really bad, he'd touch my ankle. He'd just set a hand on my ankle, and it would break my fear. Just him with his heavy old paw on my ankle."

It's then that the bad feeling comes over me. As if on cue, Pityr runs in, white as a sheet. He doesn't have to say anything. I bound back through the place and out to the drive.

She's gone with the car. With the weapons.

"No!"

He comes up beside me. "She didn't have keys—she jacked it. I thought she didn't remember..."

"*Blyad!*"

"Where will she go?" he asks.

"I don't know. It depends on what she's remembered. But I put trackers on all her shoes after she tried to escape the first time."

"Shoes. Exactly where everybody looks."

I nod. Exactly where she'd look...if her memory has returned.

CHAPTER TWENTY-FOUR

Tanechka

The Sacred River Church is hushed and beautiful. Colored light shines through stained-glass windows high above. A few faithful pray in the pews. They have no idea who has come into their midst.

I suppose I don't, either.

I go to the front and fall to my knees, making the sign of the cross. I clasp my hands together so tightly I think I might break my own bones. I feel unworthy even of looking up at Jesus. I can't remember killing all of the people I killed, but I remember begging for Viktor to fuck me.

I shut my eyes tightly, trying to gather my other sins. How can I ask forgiveness if I don't remember? How can I be washed clean?

Mother Olga said it was possible, but she didn't know what I was.

I think of Viktor. A killer like me. Familiar as a glove on my hand. At the brothel they threatened my body. Viktor threatens my very soul.

I take a spot in a pew in the front, and I whisper my prayers, bereft.

The women suffered in the brothel while I became drunk and made love with a killer. The vodka, the feel of Viktor's skin under my touch, Viktor's manhood filling me—these things I wanted.

I look up at Jesus, blurry though my tears. "Show me your light again."

Nothing.

I clutch my hands together as if I could press away the feelings I bear for Viktor. I need to find a priest. Together we'll go to the police and tell them about the brothel.

Then I'll confess.

I think of Viktor holding me. *Lisichka.* Even now I miss him.

A male voice at the end of the pew. "May I?"

My tears make his face look blurry, but I recognize the frock of the priest. "Please, Father," I say.

He slides in.

I feel instantly cold. Frightened. Is this how far I've strayed? That a priest should seem an enemy?

He says, "You are troubled."

"More than you can imagine," I say.

"Would confession help?"

"It would, Father. So much—"

He points at something over my shoulder. I look to see what he is pointing at. The confessional, perhaps?

A rustling sound behind me. Too late I turn. There's a prick on my neck. And then darkness.

* * *

I awake alone on a cold floor. If not for a sliver of light coming from the edges of a board over a high window, it would be completely dark.

He wasn't a real priest, of course.

Maybe the old Tanechka would've known. I'm good for nothing. A criminal without the helpful memories of one.

My head pounds as I sit up. Thoughts muddy. I fight my way out of my stupor enough to go to the door, nearly tripping on my skirts. I run my hands over the coarse cloth and recognize the frock as a nun's robe. Different from my old one. I wear the head scarf, too. But I'm not at the brothel; the brothel had a certain sound, a certain smell.

Somewhere else.

I try the door and find it locked. I step back unsteadily, mouth dry as a desert.

On instinct, I traverse the perimeter of the tiny room, inspecting the wall, the floor. I feel off balance.

Drugged.

I'll need to get to the window. But how?

My senses tell me this place is in a basement, and that there are men in the hall to the right, and that's also where the exit is.

I begin to see it as a colorful cube in my mind's eye, like the one Viktor put in my hands at the picnic by the lake.

The Rubik's Cube.

Move one row and new possibilities open and close. Move this other and you're surrounded. Viktor talked about that, wanting me so badly to remember. He said we'd solve standoffs the same way we solved Rubik's Cubes.

I try to remember how to be the old Tanechka, but I can't.

My body knows how to react, but I can't seem to think ahead, to form a plan. I only react. Why can't I think forward?

Footsteps. I spin. The door opens. The light blinds me.

He is there, face in the dark, light streaming in behind him. "Here she is, everybody's favorite nun. Awake at last."

It's the man who pretended to be a priest.

I can't see his face, but I remember the voice. I know he's dangerous. I was too emotional to see it before. I see it now.

He flicks on a light. Controls are outside the door. I blink. "This better?"

"Let me out."

"Yeah. Maybe not."

He walks in and shuts the door behind him. He has strange, severe looks—dark hair swept back and a nose like a beak, harsh eyes, harsh cheekbones. He might be handsome to other women in that way some severe men can be handsome, but he's not handsome to me. I can feel his evil.

"Come here." He goes to the corner table and spreads out a map. I can see from where I stand that it's Chicago. "Come on."

I cross my arms. "Will you take me back to that place? The brothel?"

"You say that almost like you want to go back," he says. "Do you want to go back?"

A question with a question. Of course. This is a man who cannot be trusted.

I do want to go back. I don't know whether I can help those women, but Viktor and his men haven't done anything.

The false priest puts a dot on the map.

"I just want to know," I say simply. "Am I going back?"

"I can tell you that there's one friend who is very eager to see you," he says. "Can you guess who?"

I ball my fists. He's speaking of Charles, the one I was forced to dine with. The man with a cockroach for a heart.

"Come, Tanechka. Can I call you Tanechka?"

I shrug.

"My name's Lazarus." He smiles.

I frown.

"You want to go back? You want to be a cheerleader for your little team there? Here's what's going to happen. You're going to tell me where you've been staying. I want to know how the guard who took you got you out of there and want to know about anybody who helped him. Extra points for addresses, license plate numbers, and vehicle makes and models."

I glare at him. He doesn't know about my connection to Viktor or Aleksio, I realize. He thinks I'm just this novice nun. Well, I am, I suppose.

"You've been gone for days. Where'd our guard have you?"

"Bring me back to that place and I'll tell you."

His lips turn up at the sides. "That's not how this works."

I shrug. "I won't tell you, then."

He stands and advances, menace in his eyes. "The sister drives a hard bargain." He comes right up to my face and adjusts my head scarf.

I flinch as five ways to kill him flash through my mind. The old Tanechka. I shut my eyes, praying for strength to be good.

"I don't think you have much of a choice here, sister. I don't want to hurt you."

"Please don't." My voice trembles. "Please don't try to hurt me."

I open my eyes and find him smiling. He thinks I'm afraid of what he'll do to me.

He has it backwards.

"Tell me what I need to know."

"No," I whisper.

A light snick tells me he holds a blade down by his side. I know the kind from the sound alone—slim unibody, with a handle that's bumpy and easy to grip and painted to resemble wood.

I've used such a blade. Not my preference, but I know it well. This isn't knowledge I wish to have. I stiffen as he touches the tip of the blade to my chin.

It's not a killing place on my neck, but it's near a killing place. One must respect the blade.

Lazarus draws his face near mine. I squeeze my eyes shut as he crowds me against the wall, the knife a needle on my chin, now. It's very near his throat, too.

I resist the impulse to take his wrist and turn the blade back on him. "You escaped from Cecil—our guard. We just need to know where he is, where he kept you."

"I won't tell you."

"I promised a certain somebody you wouldn't be harmed," he says. "Harm, though, it's a loose term, don't you think?"

My heart races. He's a trained fighter with a blade, but I have a weapon, too—surprise. I picture a move—the only one I have—a fast one-two snap designed to put the blade off me and into him.

I can't. I won't.

My eyes widen as he pushes the point of the blade into the soft flesh under my chin, breaking the skin.

Blood trickles down my neck.

"Oh dear," he whispers. "You're bleeding."

I suck in a breath, fighting the panic. Bleeding panics a person on an instinctual level. Something else I shouldn't know. He needs me; he won't hurt me. This cut is not lethal.

"Why are you protecting him?"

I close my eyes.

"Are you praying to Jesus right now?"

"Yes."

"To save you?"

I don't answer.

"Word of advice: Asking for Jesus's help is about as effective as wearing your shoe as a hat."

I say nothing.

Lazarus smirks. "Seriously. You really think he can help you right now?"

I'm not in such a good position. The trickle of blood has reached the divot at my throat.

Lazarus's gaze is cold. "I formed a question, didn't I? Voice turned up at the end and all?"

"Jesus loves even the unlovable."

"Bor-ring." Again he shifts the knife.

I keep my breathing shallow. My mind is reeling. What if Jesus wasn't showing me his beautiful eyes to get me to be a nun? What if he was just showing me love? Forgiveness?

"Location. *Now.*"

A door slams somewhere in the building, followed by a soft thud.

It's Viktor.

I know this like I know morning from night and darkness from sunshine. *We used to feel each other,* he said. *I always knew when you'd entered a building.*

Lazarus, too, knows the sound was wrong—I can tell by the look in his eyes.

A *thunk* in the hall.

"Tony?" Lazarus calls out.

Nothing.

Lazarus pulls me back into the room, away from the door, right before it bursts open.

It's Viktor. His face is bloody and he holds a man in front of him, a blade at his neck.

"The nun comes with me or this one dies," he says.

My heart pounds. He came for me.

He has one of Lazarus's men. But Lazarus has me.

"This is certainly a dilemma," Lazarus says, as though amused. "Except not."

"Behind!" I gasp as a shadow closes in behind Viktor.

Too late. A man puts a gun to Viktor's head. "Drop it," the man says.

Viktor stays, his head wound bleeding all over his face.

"Drop it or the nun dies," Lazarus says.

Viktor drops his knife. He's looking at me. He wants something from me. To move, perhaps. How?

Panic fills me. I can't think forward like that.

"Viktor," Lazarus says. "This is a nice surprise." He kicks away the knife. "Never knew you were the religious type. Or is it more of a sex thing?"

"Let her go."

Lazarus laughs. "Why would I do that?"

"You have me."

"But haven't you heard? Two birds in the hand are better than one in the bush. No? That's not how it goes?"

The man presses the gun to Viktor's head.

Lazarus drapes an arm around my shoulders and addresses Viktor. "Now, what's this lead on Kiro I've been hearing about?"

Viktor gazes at me, dark eyes shining. He's hurt—I can tell from the way he breathes. A rib, maybe. He tries to conceal it. "Gut me. Bleed me. I do not give up my brother."

"You know we only need to kill one of you for the Dragusha brother prophecy to die, and it looks to me like you're volunteering. So that's basically already happened. But why not two? I think it would make a statement. Lazarus 2.0, biotches."

The man shoves Viktor's head sideways with the gun. If he pulls the trigger, the shot will kill him. I meet his beautiful eyes.

Time seems to stop when I gaze into Viktor's eyes.

"The question is, what happens to the nun? Tell me about Kiro and I'll let her go on her merry way." He tightens his arm around my neck.

Panic flows through me, and in a flash I see the scene move forward, like a Rubik's Cube.

It all fits together in a flash. Colors turning, planes of action lining up.

And suddenly I'm moving. My elbow slides up to Lazarus's face. He regards me with shock during the split second before the pain sets in. His shock gives me what I need—the opening to remove myself from the blade while taking his hair and driving his still-stunned face into the concrete wall.

He crumples to the ground. I kick up, planting a foot in the burly man's also-stunned face. I have given Viktor the distraction he needed to take the gun.

It worked to my advantage—the helpless nun becoming a ball of fury.

"No killing," I say to him in Russian.

"Tanechka!"

"I mean it."

Viktor doesn't argue. We know how to move together. I grab the switchblade, the faux-wood handle as familiar as honey. The same make as the first blade I owned.

The memories are crashing in. I remember my childhood room. My father raising us. My mother taking tickets on the passenger rail, back and forth across the country. School in a gray cement building. Playground benches. Rides at Sky World, the feeling of flying there, lights in all colors. Something cold tugs at the edges of my mind. Another memory, cold and dark.

A gunshot rips through the air, and I spin. Viktor has the man's arm. He breaks it with a crack, and then he knocks the man out.

We move into the hall, fighting back to back.

"Hear me—no killing!" I say this in Russian as we pull out into the hall, fighting our way out.

"Blyad!" he says. "More coming up and back."

It's small, this hall. The tightness gives us the advantage of only having to take down one man each at a time. I'm still in this nun's garb. This is another advantage.

Again we fight back to back. Men come from each way. They don't shoot because if they miss us they hit one of their people.

One man comes at me with a blade, and I sever a nerve in his arm. He collapses. Very painful, but he won't die. Viktor grunts behind me, taking out more men.

The fight opens in my mind, a fast-moving grid. I move left when Viktor moves right. I track him as I finish another. He appears when I need him, knocking people out instead of killing them. We get to the small steps and run up. We get out the door. But there's something else— more wrong.

Something...something so very wrong.

Viktor wipes the blood from his eyes. My heart lurches to see him hurt. Is that it?

"Come on." He holds out his hand. I take it. We run down the broken sidewalk to a black truck.

Viktor swings open the door for me, and I climb in. He goes around and takes the wheel. My heart pounds as we scream out. I find a shirt in the back and use it to wipe the blood from his eyes.

"I got it." He snatches the shirt—he'll handle it himself. "Belt up."

I slide over to my side and click the seatbelt over me, just as he screams around a corner. Sirens behind us.

"Lazarus's cops," he growls. "Hold on. I have you."

"How did you find me?"

He wipes more blood from his eyes. "Tracker in your shoe."

Viktor. He came for me.

But something tugs at the edges of my mind. Something wrong.

A chill goes through me. In the cab of the truck, I feel a chill.

"Tanechka?" His voice sounds so far away. I hear the whoosh of wind. This chill I feel goes into my bones.

Tanechka?

He calls for me, but I'm not in the truck. I'm on top of a cliff, cold wind at my back.

I'm shaking, clinging to him, begging, crying.

Dariali Gorge.

It's Viktor, but I don't know his eyes.

Predatel! he shouts, peeling my fingers from his arm.

Cold nothingness howls at my back.

I'm begging him to believe me. I'm trying to explain about my mother.

I'm innocent, and he won't believe me.

I press my hands to my belly, remembering, feeling like I'm back there.

The cold wind. Him pulling my fingers off his arm. He shoves me backwards into the darkness of the Gorge.

I'm gasping for air. Falling. Gasping.

Before I can even think, my pika is at his throat. "It was you!"

He looks at me wildly. "Tanechka—"

The world swims before my eyes. "You thought I betrayed you? Betrayed our gang? How could you think that?"

He looks back and forth from the road to me, talking on and on. "I was wrong. I couldn't think straight. The photos—"

"I would've never betrayed you!" I can barely get the words out. "I loved you!"

My hand shakes. I'm not a killer, but I can't take my blade from his neck. A strange instinct holds it there.

"We're in trouble, Tanechka," he says. "You need to start shooting some tires or we both die."

"I was so scared, Viktor. Not about the gorge, but to be without your love. You glared at me with the eyes of a stranger! You peeled my fingers from your arms and shoved me away!"

"I know!" Blood drips from where the men hit him. "I know—I know what I did! Tanechka, if I could take it back—"

"You looked into my eyes and shoved me into the gorge like I was a piece of trash."

"I deserve to die a thousand times over for what I did. But I'm getting you out of here first."

A shot rings past.

Rage flows through me. So much rage. I don't know who I am.

"Let me at least save you," he says. "You can kill me later."

More shots.

Who the fuck is shooting at us?

Like a woman possessed, I flick the blade closed and grab the piece. I shove in the magazine, roll down the window, and twist. I shoot out the front tire of the pursuing car, and it spins out. I take another shot, and then I turn back.

He concentrates on the chase.

"Predatel?! Predatel?!" More cars are behind us. I turn and shoot, angry.

So much anger. I'm not used to it.

I hit the engine block, the tires. My aim is as sharp as cut glass, even through my rage.

"I'll do anything—"

I turn back around. "Sergei kidnapped my mother. I couldn't tell!"

"You never betrayed us, I know! I betrayed you. I betrayed *us*. It was me who should've gone into the gorge. A million times I thought it."

I freeze. "Viktor—my mother—is she…" I brace myself as he does a U-turn and then another, shooting down the sidewalk.

"Alive? Yes. I got her out."

My blood races. "She's safe?"

"I went in and grabbed her."

"How?"

"You'd be amazed what a man can do when he no longer cares for his life. I would've done anything. I still would. When I realized what I'd done, I knew saving your mother wouldn't bring you back, but I knew it's what you'd want."

"She's okay? You promise?"

"She's still in her little flat. Still complaining about the loud TV downstairs. Wearing her flowered scarves."

My pulse drums in my ears. I'm no less angry. "How she must have suffered, thinking I was dead."

"When she sees you, when she learns you're alive…you can't imagine the joy…"

"Thank you for saving her," I grate through the vengeance bubbling in my heart.

"The debt I have to you will never be repaid."

"Konstantin—"

"Dead." One clipped word. His face is stone.

I suck in a breath. "*Mne ochen zhal.*"

"Thank you."

I gaze out the window. A passing strip mall. All the American brands with their colors and confidence.

He slows. Our pursuers are nowhere in sight. We've lost them.

Lost everything.

CHAPTER TWENTY-FIVE

Viktor

She doesn't attack me.

"Tanechka?"

She stares out the window. She seems lost. A little bit wild. Is she biding her time?

In a strange voice, she says, "Bring me to the brothel. We will free those women now."

I tell her we're working on it, almost ready to pounce, but not yet.

She frowns. "Bring me to Nikki, then."

"Why? Why Nikki?"

"You said you'd do anything. Bring me to Nikki."

I call Aleksio, still at Konstantin's place. I tell him I have Tanechka.

"Good." He lowers his voice. "Stay away. Too many cops." He tells me Nikki is staying at Tito's place.

I head for Tito's.

Tanechka's silence is worse than her recriminations. I need her to do something. Anything.

I need her to end this pain. Only she can end this pain.

"I'm sorry about Konstantin." Her voice sounds far off. "He was like a father to you, I know."

I don't understand why she's being kind. Is she toying with me? Making me wait? Tanechka used to toy with people.

"He was a father mostly to Aleksio," I say. "I knew him only a year."

She looks out the window. "A year can run deep."

* * *

Tito's place is a brownstone on the North Side. Nikki's already expecting us—she's the only one around, except for the P.I.'s large black-and-white dog. I wash and bandage my head wound in the bathroom. The wound stings. Perversely, I'm glad.

I go back to Tito's kitchen and call Aleksio again. I need to hear his voice, to know he's okay. I don't like that he's out in the open while he's grieving. This is a dangerous time. He assures me Tito's on the fringes managing security.

Tanechka is back with a duffel bag. "Sit." She sets it on the floor.

I sit. "What's in there?"

"A surprise."

Warily, I sit.

In a flash, she has my arms cuffed to the metal chair back.

I lurch up, chair and all, swinging wildly, trying to wrench free. I succeed only in smashing cupboards.

She and Nikki grab the chair. They anchor me to the floor with their combined weight. Nikki cuffs each of my ankles to each leg as the dog barks. Then she tapes me.

Wildly I look up, yanking at my restraints. "What are you doing? I won't be tied."

"We need to take those women out of the brothel," she says calmly.

"You can't. We have a plan for them!" I say. "We'll get them out."

"I am weary of your words."

"Don't do it."

She gives me a hard look. "We'll call the police after we have the women out," she says.

Nikki hauls a semiautomatic from the duffel, dark hair swinging around her shoulders. "How do you use this?"

"You don't." Tanechka takes it from her. "No killing."

"You're going to take that place down without killing anybody?" I say. "Without me? No. You can't."

"We can," she says. "All that time when I was in there, I could've broken out of that little room at any time. I should've pulled those girls out weeks ago. I didn't re-member, but I do now." She turns to Nikki. "You know where Tito keeps his toolbox?"

"Basement utility room. Last door on the left," Nikki says.

Tanechka takes a 9mm from the pack and hands it to Nikki. "Watch him. Yell if he tries to get free. The chair won't hold him; it'll only slow him down." Tanechka strolls out.

"This is suicide," I say to Nikki once we're alone.

"No talking." She stands across the kitchen from me and studies the black glittery nails of her non-gun hand, hair falling once again in her eyes.

After a while, I nod at the 9mm in her hand. "You know how to handle one of those, but how well?"

She snorts and looks away. A brave front. The shape of her brave front shows me she is frightened.

"You can't do this, just you two," I say. "Tanechka's not thinking straight—she does big things when she's upset. You and her can't do this alone."

Nikki flicks her hair from her eyes. "I'm not worried. Tito told me all about her."

"You didn't even like her before."

She shrugs, the cool little street urchin. "I sure as fuck like her now."

"You need to hear me. You need to trust me."

"Yeah, yeah, yeah," she says. "That would hold more weight if you hadn't tried to cut off Mira's finger and kill your girlfriend."

Tanechka's back. She slings an assault rifle around her shoulder. "Hurry. The switchover time is soon."

"What's switchover time?" I ask.

"You are not in this."

"Let me back you up. Let us be a team. Let me take the dangerous parts."

Nikki heads for the door with the duffel bag. "Tell Tito *yo* for me and whatever you do, don't let the dog out."

"Let me kill for you," I say. "I'll take it all on myself, all the darkness. Let me take it all on for you."

Tanechka turns back, eyes shining. "Too late." She walks out and leaves me.

Wildly I jerk my arms, jerking at the joints of the chair. I can't let her go—she really isn't thinking straight. The chair is metal, but it's held together with little screws. I only have to be stronger than those screws. I focus my mind on getting out, and not on the bleak reality of everything.

Because if I look too hard, I see Konstantin, our guiding light, dead in his foyer.

I see one brother bereft. My other brother in grave danger.

I see our Russian allies turning on us, becoming dangerous enemies.

And I see the woman I love, not quite herself yet. And she's walking into a fight she can't win.

CHAPTER TWENTY-SIX

Tanechka

Our raid on the virgin brothel starts out well.

We park the SUV in the back, keys in, doors unlocked. I hotwire a van and get it running.

We get there with five minutes to spare before the guards have their staff meeting at switchover time—in a windowless room with a door that can be bolted from the outside. It was converted from one of the women's room. The bolt they keep taped open. It will be so easy to imprison them. They'll see how it feels.

We wait in the bushes at the front of the place. The staff room is the second door in the front.

"We have this," I tell her. "These guards are soft, sloppy."

She nods, but I can see Viktor wobbled her a bit.

We go over the plan. We'll slip the knockout gas canister in and bolt the door. Nikki will keep cover behind the line of metal lockers in the hallway and shoot low when she sees shadows underneath.

She nods. She is not relaxed enough.

"Your part of this operation will be like a video game. See a shadow and shoot," I say.

She nods.

"But if they start to escape, if you feel scared, you end it, just like a video game. You run. You'll help me most by running if things go wrong. Do you understand?"

Again she nods.

"They'll be slow in their thinking from the knockout gas, and you'll have the mask. They're more scared of you than you are of them."

She smiles uncertainly. "That's what they say about bears."

"With that gun you are more dangerous than any bear." Simple truth.

When the time comes, I take the canister of gas from Tito's duffel and make her hold it for me. The writing on it is Hungarian, but the ingredients I recognized when I saw it in Tito's basement.

We hide the duffel in some bushes with some extra weapons, just in case. I steal up and pick the front door lock, and we slip in.

The hallway is dark, hushed. Voices inside the room. The smell of pickled cabbage. Quiet as a mouse, I pull the tape from the bolt and make sure it slides. I ease the door open. I gesture to Nikki to put the mask over her nose and mouth.

I pull my scarf over my mouth and nose, snap the canister open, and roll it in.

I slam the door and bolt it.

There's no time to wait to see what happens. I start down the hall.

I unbolt the door of Natasha's room just as the shots start. Natasha is one of the most capable of the women here. "There's a black SUV and an idling van outside," I tell her in Russian. "Help me free everyone and get them out. Don't wait for me if there's trouble."

"What's the shooting?"

"The shooter's with me. We locked the guards in the break room."

She gets going. Next I free Mavis, the most bossy of the women. I give her the same speech and lead her to the back, propping the door open. "Two vehicles. Fifteen in each. You figure it out with Natasha."

She nods.

I go back in. There's a faint smell from the gas, but not so bad with the front and back doors open. My old brothel mates are surprised to see me, frightened of the shooting, but everybody's orderly. Ten minutes it takes. A quick operation.

The first van rolls off, then the second. The women are out just like that. Easy.

Or so I think.

Not all of the guards were in the staff room, as it turns out.

I didn't know that.

I go back in and hear something in the TV room. I think maybe Nikki or a woman is hiding there, and I go in.

That's when the small group of guards ambushes me.

I take two without killing—both knocked out against the refrigerator. This is the beauty of the nun's outfit—the element of surprise.

When they stop treating me as a nun, I pull out my weapons, one in each hand.

By the end, I hold two men at gunpoint. And they hold me.

A double Mexican standoff.

One of Viktor's and my worst nightmares. There was no good solution for such a situation. No Rubik's Cube way out.

Only crazy ideas.

And I haven't yet called the police, told them all these culprits are locked in a room. I should've done it.

Shots from the front of the building. Nikki. How are the guards in there still awake? But I have worse problems here in the TV room.

The rules of a double Mexican standoff are obvious, but it never hurts to state them. I want the guards to understand this situation as I do. "If you so much as move, I pull both triggers," I say. "If you shoot, I pull both triggers. If one of you drops, I pull both triggers."

All bluffs, of course.

"Open your hands and we won't hurt you," the guard with freckles says. He's on my left.

"If I open my hands, I'm dead," I say. "So then, why not take both of you with me?"

No good solution. We all know this.

I take a deep breath.

I'm shaking deep inside, but I know how to conceal it. So much information pouring back into my head. So much emotion, destroying the peace I felt with the sisters.

"If you open your hands and drop your guns, I'll let you live," I say.

"Fuck that," the other one says.

They don't believe me. They look at me, and they see a killer. They would've been right once. Did they not see my refusal to kill? I knocked out those men. I did not kill.

Viktor is wrong about many things. But he's right about one thing: This takeover couldn't be accomplished without bloodshed. I wouldn't be in this standoff if I'd killed carelessly and easily, as the old Tanechka would have.

All of the possible moves and outcomes run through my mind. Most end with Nikki and me dying. A few end with just me dying.

That's the option I choose. I call out to Nikki. "Get out, Nikki!"

The two men watch me warily.

Nikki's voice: "I'm good where I am."

"Nikki!" But the argument takes precious attention.

I need her to go. At this point, not much changes, even if all of the guards wake up and get out. I'll still have a standoff with all the guards. Me against all the guards.

Two is only a little bit better than that.

There was a time, back when Viktor and I were so wild and free, that we would've felt excited by such a thing.

The standoff goes on.

I stare straight ahead, keeping them both in my sight with what peripheral vision I have. Monitoring people on either side of you is part concentration and part relaxation.

More shots. I calculate the shots she has left across the three weapons I left her with. Not so many.

At one point the guards look at one another.

They could coordinate. I don't have the sense that they've worked together long, but they could find a way. They're in a far better position than I am. Do they understand that?

Viktor and I used to spend hours dissecting scenarios like this. We always assumed everybody did, until we learned otherwise—that we were *nerds* about it, as the Americans might say.

I remember everything now.

I remember everything I knew as Tanechka and everything I knew as a novice nun. I contain all of it.

Another gunshot rings out from the break room. Nikki. Holding them in.

She doesn't understand—she won't survive this if she stays. She can't see ahead the way Viktor and I can. Viktor and I trained ourselves to think ahead about all of those Rubik's Cube moves.

Every move affects another, unseen and seen.

A double Mexican standoff like this was the worst. Neither of us had ever been in one, but we'd imagined it.

And now here I am.

We'd heard of one in Vladivostok that lasted hours. It ended from muscle failure. The older fighter couldn't hold his weapon up any longer. Standing here with my arms out to either side, all the tension and adrenaline pumping through me, I can see how that would happen.

Viktor and I decided that you could never win such a standoff alone. You could only win such a standoff with an external helper, and that helper would die. "The replacement move," we called it.

I think of the diagrams we used to scribble.

There was such beauty in what we had. I remember every kiss. I remember everything we dreamed. I remember that picnic in Gorky Park. I remember Red Square and my Taylor Swift outfit. I remember his face as he choked down the sweet Manhattan cocktail while I laughed.

I remember walking around Moscow with no money in our jacket pockets. I remember the bubbles in the pink champagne. I remember being bloody together. Happy together.

And I remember his eyes the day he threw me over the cliff. Like my own heart, cast from my body.

And I remember the peace I felt when I didn't remember it.

I sigh, clearing my mind. Alone in a double Mexican. I wish Viktor could see, so he would know, considering this was such a topic of interest for us. *Look at me, you* kozel, I'd joke. *I'm going to die in a double Mexican standoff. So much more glorious than your gorge. Your paltry Daliani Gorge.*

I smile.

"What?" one of the guards says.

I laugh. "My nines weigh half what your .357s weigh. One of you will tire first. One will move. One jerk and we go. We do this."

A creak from the back door.

I stare straight ahead, watching both of them and neither of them. My pulse races.

He's come.

Everything in the world shifts. Gravity itself seems to shift.

Viktor.

Another creak. My heart pounds as he nears.

He appears at the door, eyes burning into mine. Instantly, he sees all. He smiles, Glocks in both his hands. "Imagine this, *lisichka.*"

"Put them down, on the floor!" the one on my right yells. He's agitated, and an agitated man will sometimes shoot when he doesn't mean to.

Viktor puts his hands up, still holding the guns. He addresses me in Russian. "One solution."

I widen my eyes when I realize what he's proposing. "*Nyet,*" I whisper.

"What did he say?" one of the guards asks. "No Russian."

"The replacement move. We've thought this through," Viktor continues in Russian.

"This is my operation," I say. "My operation, my decision. Go find Nikki and take her away."

"Are you crazy? We'll finally see if it works."

My blood races. As the fourth person, he would dive at me and replace me. We worked it out precisely. It's true.

There are certain mechanical eye-hand principles you understand when you are us.

One of them is how to draw men's hands this way and that. The motion of the one who dives in draws the gunfire away from the center person. It's the diver who gets the bullets.

In one of our plans, the external helper wore a vest and helmet. A suit of armor. Viktor, of course, wears only his suit.

Another more advanced idea was that he, as diver, could fly at me, spinning in the air, shooting. The three of them would shoot each other. He takes the bullets and shoots the bullets as he flattens me to the ground, protecting me with his body. Or vice versa, if I were the diver.

In Russian, he says. "You don't have a choice. I'm the diver. I'm going to replace you with myself. Go back and find your peace, your Jesus."

"*Viktor.*"

"I tried to kill you. This is how it ends."

Something inside of me agrees—an eye for an eye. That's what I believed in as Tanechka.

Only his death will right the wrong that he did.

I look at him—really look at him. I look at him with my whole heart, feeling my love for him.

My love for him is sweet and bright. In a flash, I feel something better come over me—forgiveness.

I forgive him. The sisters taught me how to have a big heart, big enough to forgive.

I couldn't have forgiven him before.

But my heart is big enough now. "*Ya tebe proshchayu,* Viktor."

He looks stunned. His whisper is hoarse—"I don't deserve your forgiveness."

"Of course you deserve it. I love you."

He looks stunned. Uncomprehending. "What about Jesus?"

"I have room for both Jesus and you."

"Jesus is just fairy tales to me."

"I don't care."

"I'll shoot if you say one more word in Russian!" the older guard says. An empty threat. The guard won't shoot unless he has to.

"You forgive me?"

"Yes, *pryanichek!*" Gingerbread man, it means. A name I used to call him when he was being a baby.

"I tried to kill you!"

I smile. "Yeah, you really fucked it up."

He blinks, speaks in a voice so soft. "I love you so much. But look where we are. We can't have all things now."

"No."

"Remember how we visualized it? Like the Olympic team, we visualized this over and over. Remember?"

I shake my head. "Don't do it."

"Don't you see what a gift it is? I threw you off the cliff," he says. "I didn't believe in our love, and I killed you. You remember how you clung to me?"

"But I forgive you, Viktor."

"Do you know how that feels? To have your for-giveness? To take your place? The pain begins to move."

"Save Nikki and let me handle this. Respect my choices for once," I growl in Russian.

"I am respecting your choices. I didn't have faith in you before, but I do now. Having faith in you means support-ing you in all that you choose for yourself, even your life in the convent."

I shake my head, fighting the tears.

"We used to wonder whether the two might even shoot each other," he says. "Remember?"

"Fantasies."

"*Lisichka*—"

I begin to laugh. "We're arguing over who dies. We promised never to do that, *pryanichek*."

He smiles. "You said, 'Shoot me if we ever argue about who dies in a standoff.' And then I said, 'No, shoot me if we argue about who dies in a standoff.'"

In Russian, I say, "You're going to make me cry and destroy my peripheral vision, you jerk."

"Tell Kiro I love him," Viktor says. "Tell him that I wish I could have met him, and tell Aleksio I love him. He always says we Russians are so fucking dramatic. What would he say about this?"

"Viktor."

His face goes serious. "I never stopped loving you."

"*Ya tebya lyublyu*," I tell him. "I love you." There's a lump in my throat. I have him back, and now he's going to do this.

He doesn't telegraph—he flies at me.

It's as if he comes in slow motion.

I see everything. His beautiful face with his big jaw, clenched and determined. The sweet little dimple. The twist of his shoulders as he begins the spin, midair. Arms out. I see the flash of the gun barrels as they reflect the ceiling light. The blast.

The weight of him knocks the air from me. I go bone-less, arms out. I feel the bullets hit him, feel the violent impact of them on his big body before we hit the floor.

Everything goes quiet.

Except for Viktor, a great weight on my chest, breath labored.

"Viktor!" I ease out from under him. My chest is wet with blood—his blood. Blood on my hands. Blood every-where. The two guards are dead.

I kneel over him. He looks up at me hazily.

"*Pryanichek.*" I rip apart his shirt.

There's a big hole in his chest. Too big. Too big for his heart. Too big for life.

I press a hand to his chest. "Don't you die on me, Viktor!" Maybe it's his heart. Maybe not.

"You love me still," he whispers. "You forgave me."

Shots. "Nikki!" I call.

Nothing.

He's losing so much blood. "I forgive you, yes, but only if you fight. Only if you stay alive." I adjust my hand on his chest. I press a hand to his cheek, keep contact with his gaze. He's sweating. But his skin is cold.

He still sees me, though. It's good—when they don't die immediately, there's hope.

Nikki arrives. "Fuck." I hear her call 911.

Viktor needs help sooner.

"Can you walk? Do we move you or wait? What happens if we help you to the car?"

Sometimes you can ask the wounded such things. Sometimes when life is on the line, they get such clarity.

"Yes. Let's try."

Nikki and I pull him up and get him down the hall. It's slow, and his breathing doesn't sound right. A collapsed lung.

We get out of the building, down two steps that didn't seem so bad before. I spot Viktor's car. "There. The Navigator."

"Keys, right pocket," he gasps.

Nikki grabs them and opens the back door for us. Viktor stumbles in and flops sideways, taking the whole seat. I wedge myself into the little space between the back seat and the back of the front seat, crouching between. I press my hand to his chest. "You think you can take the whole seat?" I joke.

Viktor groans as the car peels out. Nikki drives like hell to the hospital.

"Will he make it?" she asks, screaming around a corner.

"He better. He owes me," I say.

He stares up at me. Anguish in his eyes. He wants to apologize again.

"Shhh," I say. "They shot each other like we imagined. Can you believe it?"

Soon enough, his eyes start getting unfocused. He tries to help me press his chest.

"I have you," I say.

I press his chest like it's my own heart.

Because it is.

CHAPTER TWENTY-SEVEN

Viktor

S he's there like an angel, holding my hand. Everything around her is bright and hazy. I think she is an
angel.

I try to smile, but tubes going out of my mouth stop
me. I lift my arms to take them out, but she has my wrists.
"Be still, *pryanichek*."

She calls out to Aleksio. He's here?

I try to say her name, but my mouth feels like it's
stuffed with cotton.

"Shh. You're going to be okay."

I'm alive? How can it be?

But I am.

I'm alive, and she's sitting at my bedside. She drizzles a
bit of water into my mouth. I swallow it down. I search
her face. She drizzles some more.

"You forgave me," I whisper.

"Yes."

I try to sit up, but the pain twists through me.

"Stop it. The doctor says you'll have to stay in bed for two weeks straight, and already you're trying to leave."

"You're here."

She frowns. "Yes." This as though I've said something so obvious.

"Why didn't you go to the convent?"

"And miss my chance to chain you to a radiator by your ankle? What do you think? A nice ankle cuff?"

"You need to go. The convent is your heart's desire. It's not too late. You were happy there."

She strokes a hand over my forehead. "The best parts I carry with me."

She won't go back?

"I want to go back," she says, reading my face. "But I want to go back with you. To bring you, to show you. Maybe after we all find Kiro?"

After we all find Kiro.

I don't know if the tightness in my chest is from the bullet ravaging me or from Tanechka forgiving me. Talking like part of the family.

She leans down to kiss my cheek. Figures loom behind her. I squint as Aleksio comes into view.

"The bullet just missed your heart." He kneels at my side. "You scared us."

Yuri's there, arm in a sling. "They shot each other. You and Tanechka are officially insane."

My laugh feels like it rips my chest open.

"Stop," Tanechka say softly.

My awareness expands out, and my mind clicks back online. Armed men stand around the edges of the room. I remember the war. We're in a hospital, but it's not safe here. A doctor muscles through.

"Kiro," I try to say.

"We'll find him, don't worry. We're on it. The Dragusha brothers will be together. Even you can't fuck that up with your insane choreography. Have I ever told you Russians are way too fucking dramatic?"

I try to reply.

"Don't make him talk." Tanechka takes out a tube of lip moisturizer and smooths it onto my lips.

I feel light. Like a weight off.

Suddenly I know things will turn out with these people I love at my side. I believe that we'll find Kiro. I believe in our family.

I believe that someday Tanechka and I will go lie on the hillock in Donetsk and visit with her sisters there and her goats.

I have faith in her. I have faith our love.

EPILOGUE

Viktor

Tanechka stretches out in front of the fire on the bearskin rug.

She wears jeans and her favorite Ramones T-shirt, eyeliner thick around her pretty blue eyes, blonde hair splayed out.

"Another," she says, opening her mouth.

I toss another lemon jelly into her mouth from where I am in the chair. It sails through her teeth and lands on her tongue.

"My aim is perfect," I say. "As usual."

She rolls her eyes, but I know she thinks it's hot when I'm good at things. And I'm good at very many things.

She sucks on the treat. She's been making up for lost time with the sweets. Lemon cake every night. Pink champagne at lunch.

I shift with difficulty. My chest is bandaged. I'm not supposed to be out of bed, but Tanechka and I, we were never so good at following rules.

She hasn't forgotten about the convent. She Skypes with the sisters a lot. She has made me come on Skype to meet Mother Olga, a severe old woman with eyes like night. I played the nice boyfriend for the computer screen, but Mother Olga just glowered. She knows who I am.

It's okay. She loves Tanechka, still, even though Tanechka will never be a nun. I sometimes suspect that the only person who thought Tanechka could be a nun was Tanechka.

I used to think that the nuns stole something from Tanechka. Blotted out her true heart. But in the end, they helped to make her heart bigger. Gave her something new.

She insists on going to church every Sunday, though. This is something my brother has a hard time understanding, but I get it. Tanechka has always made her own crazy rules.

And she fucks and fights and drinks and loves and laughs as much as she ever did.

More, maybe.

And she forgave me. I thought death was the only thing that could end the pain of what I did to her. I was wrong.

So it's all good, as Mira likes to say.

"Another," she says.

I draw another lemon jelly from the wrinkled bag and toss. It traces an arc and lands in her mouth.

She chews. The fire crackles behind her.

Mira's coming over later this afternoon. She and Tanechka have plans to walk the lake. They make an interesting pair, Mira so serious and Tanechka so wild. They balance each other.

Aleksio will stay with me. We'll drink and talk about Kiro. It's taking too long to find him. We both think it all the time, but we don't say it aloud.

She turns to me. Something new in her smile.

I snort. "If you think I'll let you suck my cock with that sour lemon mouth, think again."

"You sure?" She begins to crawl toward me.

I'm laughing. "Tanechka."

She rests her hands on my thighs, grinning up at me, challenge in her eyes. "I think you'd like my sour lemon mouth."

I shove my hands into her hair and grab two fistfuls.

I'll love her sour lemon mouth.

I'll love her forever.

~The End~

Acknowledgements

I'm so grateful to my brilliant husband for his brain-storming help—and his understanding while I was way too consumed with writing this book. I also want to hugely thank my wonderful critique partners – Amber Belldene, Joanna Chambers, Carolyn Jewel, Katie Reus, and Skye Warren. These authors provided smart, generous feedback and ideas, and read this book when it was in utter scary mayhem.

Thank you also to Christin Ostheimer, who helped me immensely with her Russian language and culture knowledge. Editor Deb Nemeth provided brilliant developmental editing and copy editing. Sadye of Fussy Librarian did an incredible job of proofreading and so far beyond. (Any mistakes are my own last minute changes.) I'm also massively grateful to all of you wonderful bloggers, Facebook book-lovers, tweeters, and readers who so generously pitched in to bring love to this series. I want to kiss you all!

Thank you also to Heather Roberts of Social Butterfly PR—you are keeping me sane in so many ways! And thanks to BookBeautiful for the gorgeous cover. Kisses to my reader friends in the Annika Martin Fabulous Gang. I am just so grateful to be surrounded by such an amazing community of readers and writers.

About Annika

I love writing dirty stories about dangerous criminals, hanging out with my man and my two cats, and kicking snow clumps off the bottom of cars around Minneapolis. I've had tons of jobs: factory worker, waitress at a zillion different places, shop clerk, advertising writer. Animals are a huge passion of mine, especially whales and lost dogs. I like to run and read books in bed, and I spend way too much time in coffee shops. In my spare time I write as the RITA award-winning author Carolyn Crane.

I love hearing from you and hanging out!

- ❖ Email me at annika@annikamartinbooks.com
- ❖ Visit annikamartinbooks.com to find out about the   latest news and to get on my newsletter.
- ❖ You are warmly invited to join my facebook group, the fabulous gang at: facebook.com/groups/AnnikaMartinFabulousGang/
- ❖ My facebook page is: facebook.com/AnnikaMartinBooks
- ❖ And twitter! twitter.com/Annika_Martin

Books by Annika Martin

Dangerous Royals
Dark Mafia Prince
Wicked Mafia Prince
Savage Mafia Prince

Romantic Comedy
Most Eligible Billionaire

Taken Hostage by Kinky Bank Robbers
The Hostage Bargain (Book 1 of Taken Hostage by
Kinky Bank Robbers)
The Wrong Turn (Book #2 of Taken Hostage by
Kinky Bank Robbers)
The Deeper Game (Book #3 of Taken Hostage by
Kinky Bank Robbers)
Taken Hostage by Kinky Bank Robbers: the 3-book set
The Most Wanted (Book #4 of Taken Hostage by
Kinky Bank Robbers)

Criminals & Captives
PRISONER
by Annika Martin & Skye Warren
HOSTAGE
by Annika Martin & Skye Warren

Writing as Carolyn Crane

Sexy, gritty romantic suspense
Against the Dark (Book #1 of the Associates)
Off the Edge (Book #2 of the Associates)
Into the Shadows (Book #3 of the Associates)
Behind the Mask (Book #4 of the Associates)

Plotty, twisty-turny urban fantasy
Mind Games (Book 1 of the Disillusionists)
Double Cross (Book 2 of the Disillusionists)
Head Rush (Book 3 of the Disillusionists)
Plus assorted shorts and single titles

More about Carolyn's
books: http://authorcarolyncrane.com

Made in the USA
San Bernardino,
CA